A HEART OF SECRETS AND SHADOWS
A TALE OF LEVANTHRIA

A.P BESWICK

CARA CLARE

A.P BESWICK
PUBLICATIONS

ISBN - 978-1-916671-19-5

Edited by - Quinn Nichols - Quill And Bone Editing

Cover Design - Rafido Design

FOREWORD

A Heart Of Secrets And Shadows is a dark fantasy romance, a genre of writing I am relatively new to. I did not want that to deter me from telling a story that further builds on the lore and the ever growing world of Levanthria. For this reason I enlisted the help of best selling fantasy and paranormal romance writer Cara Clare to help me bring this dark retelling to life.

ACKNOWLEDGMENTS

This story is for all those readers who asked for a Levanthria story with just a hint of spice. It is still a dark retelling, just with a focus on an even darker romance.

I

CALLA

The ocean's briny scent fills my nostrils as I stare down at the bustling docks below. Usually, the ocean is where I come to feel calm. At peace.

Today, her waves bring nothing but ripples of anxiety to the shore of my ribs.

I close my eyes and inhale deeply, willing the clamour of the crowd to fade. Pretending I am alone in the precious solitude of my chambers – still a million minutes away from the fate that now draws closer.

My efforts are hopeless.

Beneath a cloudy sky, the churning water mimics the swirl of fear in my gut as Prince Edmund's ship draws closer.

It is undoubtedly a magnificent vessel, a true leviathan, and my father's covetous eyes glisten as he stares at her. She is far grander than any of *our* ships.

With her painted sides, a shade of navy that bleeds into the ocean's hue, and her billowing sails, this boat is the embodiment of everything mine and Edmund's union is designed to facilitate.

Power. Riches. Ambition.

Of course, it is being sold to our citizens as a union that will secure the *safety* of both kingdoms. But it is not the safety of the people that concerns my father; it is the safety of his name. His legend. His place in the history books.

He puffs out his chest and smooths his palms over his velvet waistcoat. At his side, my mother barely moves. She is a dutiful statue. Placid and compliant. She knows her place.

I twist my hands together in front of my stomach as dread solidifies in my gut. The crowd is growing increasingly jubilant, but as their energy builds, the urge to run becomes almost overwhelming.

"Princess, how do you feel about meeting Prince Edmund?" someone yells from the gaggle of people in front of the guards.

I smile and nod in reply.

We are separated from the crowd by a raised platform and our armed guards. But while I feel obliged to respond to the compliments and questions that are thrown my way, my father ignores any attempts to greet him or make eye contact.

He is focused only on Edmund's boat.

As trumpets sound, announcing the boat's arrival at the docks, my father's lips stretch into a greed-filled smile. The prow of Edmund's ship is a masterpiece of craftsmanship, adorned with the elaborate, gilded figurehead of a lion. A symbol of the strength and nobility of Edmund's house and the kingdom of Xandor.

"Do you see the gold, Calla?" My father turns to meet my gaze.

I nod silently.

"Soon, that gold will be yours. You will stand at the prow of Prince Edmund's ship, run your fingers over her carvings, and know you are queen of everything you see before you."

I turn back towards the ocean. Gold leaves glint along the

lion's mane and the curve of its snarling muzzle. But I have never wanted gold; all I have ever wanted is freedom.

"Soon, we will be lions too," my father says, his voice cracking with anticipation. "Zakron will be great once again."

A sigh strains against the bodice of my dress, but I do not let it rise to my lips.

Zakron. Historically weak, we are to be made stronger through marriage.

My marriage.

To a man I have never met.

It is my duty as princess to do as my father commands. It is my duty to put my people above myself.

So why do I feel like I am betraying them?

"Princess . . ." A deep, familiar voice slides like velvet over my skin.

My heart swells, and warmth spreads down my limbs. If my cheeks were not covered with powder to smooth my complexion, it would be clear to all who surround me that I am blushing.

This is the effect he has on me – the effect he has always had.

"Thorne." I do not look at him, simply nod and keep my gaze focused on the gilded lion that approaches our shore. But I do not need to look at him to *feel* him.

Slotting himself between me and my father, Thorne allows his fingertips to graze mine. My breath catches in my chest. Electricity skitters up my arm.

How do they not see it? All these people, gathered to watch the prince's arrival . . . how do they not see the way my skin lights up, and the way the air shimmers with heat, when Thorne is close by?

Finally, I look at him. He glances down at me. He is tall with thick dark hair that settles on his shoulders. His lips twitch, but he does not allow them to curl into a smile; that is something he reserves only for me in our most private moments.

To the rest of the world, he is an arrogant, lonely bachelor. My father's devoted aide. A man of strict morals and pious ambition.

To me, he is everything.

The sun, the moon, and all the spaces in between.

He is everything, and yet he is nothing because he can never be mine.

"The prince is almost with us," Thorne says, speaking to my father.

"Indeed." My father claps Thorne hard on the shoulder and nods at him. "You'll greet him. See he's escorted to the palace in style —"

I'm trying to listen to Thorne and my father's conversation, but something catches my eye in the crowd. A young girl with ink-black hair, waving at me. She is painfully thin and there are dark shadows beneath her eyes. One so young should not have shadows like that.

My chest constricts angrily. These people think the union of our two kingdoms will ease their strife. But I know my father. His newfound riches will line his pockets and decorate his palaces. But they will not reach the hands or mouths of the people who need them the most.

As for Edmund . . . I know nothing of what *he* intends to do when he finally has a wife and is crowned king. But from what I have heard, he is more concerned with jewels and playthings than politics.

"Princess . . ." the girl's mother calls to me. "My daughter loves you so much. She's been very sick. Might you spare a moment?"

I move towards the mother, and the girl's face visibly brightens.

My guard, Erik, watches carefully. I nod to tell him it's all right. Slowly, he steps aside and allows the mother and child onto the platform.

I crouch down and clasp my hands around the girl's. "What's your name?" I ask.

"Raven," she replies, blinking up at me.

"Hi, Raven."

"You're so very beautiful," she whispers.

I smile and shake my head. "Beauty comes from in here," I tell her, pressing my palm to her tiny chest.

The girl starts to cry. She mutters something I can't understand, then tugs away from me. I rise to my feet and take her mother's hand. "I'm sorry. I hope I didn't upset her."

"Oh, no, princess." The mother meets my eyes. "She really does admire you. She's just upset because of what's about to happen."

For a moment, I assume she is talking about my marriage to the prince. But then something about the tone of her voice snags in my mind. I frown, trying to understand what it is that is bothering me. Before I can speak, she has pulled a blade from her skirt.

I raise my hands, but she launches herself towards me.

The tip of her knife sears my upper arm, slicing through my silk sleeve and drawing blood. She is screaming profanity at me. The girl is screaming too.

The crowd thickens and the guards leap into action. Half are pushing back the crowd, the other half are surrounding my father. None comes for me.

5

The woman lunges again, but then two thick hands take hold of her shoulders. The knife is knocked from her grasp. Thorne stands behind her. Meeting my eyes, he pins her tight to his chest so her back is pressed against him. She claws at his arm, but he is bigger and stronger.

With his free hand, he draws his dagger. He whispers something in her ear, still staring into my eyes.

And then he draws his blade across her throat.

As she crumples to the floor, I press my fingers to the wound on my arm, surprised by the blood. There is more. My hand is drenched. My face is wet. But it is not my blood, it is hers.

I look down at my chest to see scarlet beads dripping down between my breasts.

Raven's mother lies at my feet, neck oozing, eyes wide and reflecting the grey clouds above us. Thorne towers above her. His face is dark as thunder. He wipes his blade on his cloak, then sheaths it.

I stumble backwards, and Thorne catches me before I fall.

"What did I do . . .? Why would she . . .?" I whisper.

Thorne stares into my eyes. His jaw twitches with anger. But he does not answer my question, simply helps me stand and bellows to the crowd, "There is nothing to see here!"

Understanding they are not supposed to be staring or whispering, the wide-eyed spectators immediately turn away from the platform. They are eerily quiet, their heartbeats almost palpable in the air around us.

I am trembling. My arm hurts, but the sting of the woman's blood hurts more. It feels too hot and too slick on my skin, and I am almost overwhelmed by the urge to scrub it free.

My father pushes through the throng of guards, grabs my wrist, and squeezes hard. "What did you do?" he spits, yanking me away from Thorne.

"I . . . she . . . the child . . ."

"How could you be so reckless? So stupid?"

I search for Thorne but he is avoiding my gaze. He hates it when my father speaks to me like this, and I long for the day he forgets himself and comes to my aid. Except, that would be the end of both of us.

"What *happened*, Calla?" my father hisses.

"I don't know," I whisper.

Except I do know. I know that his citizens aren't as in favour of mine and Edmund's great union as he would like to believe. I have heard the whispers because *I* listen.

For a moment, I imagine a world in which I am able to speak the truth. In which I stand up to my father, and the people rally behind me, and a new age dawns.

But that is the stuff of fairy stories, and my life is no story.

Rage swells in my father's gaze as he takes in my now-bloodstained clothes. He bites his lower lip, which is almost swallowed by his thick grey beard. "You cannot meet the prince like this. Go to the docks, give him a glimpse of what he's come here for but *do not* get too close. Leave before he disembarks."

"I could change . . ." I glance back at my carriage which always contains a chest of spare clothes.

"You will meet him at the banquet," my father says bluntly. He does not move, doesn't close the gap between us or tighten his grip on my arm. But I know the iterations of his face. I can read them like a map, and the twitch of his eyes tells me I am veering too close to petulance for his liking.

I lower my gaze and slide my hands into the pockets of my robes.

He turns on his heels, beckoning to his guards. As he marches away, the crowd parting like butter to the knife of his stride, I hold my breath and push back my shoulders.

7

I can feel Thorne's simmering presence beside me. I glance at him, and when our gazes collide, tears spring to my eyes. He has never seen me cry. Today will not be the day my weakness bubbles to the surface.

"I will be by your side tonight," he whispers, moving his fingers to gently brush the inside of my wrist. "Everything will be okay, Calla."

"No," I whisper. "It won't." I turn and look up at him. "Because I am marrying the wrong man."

We descend from the cliffs to the docks. It is quieter here; the citizens of Zakron have been instructed to stay up high and not to crowd the prince on his arrival.

His ship slows her pace, her grand sails billowing like the wings of a swan in flight. She is almost upon us and, around me, the pageantry of Edmund's arrival continues to unfold.

Silk banners, emblazoned with both my family's crest and that of Edmund's, snap in the bracing wind while musicians tune their instruments, their discordant twangs soon to be moulded into a welcoming symphony. Nobles – the only ones allowed to gather at the docks – jostle for position, their finery a riot of colour and their jewels a testament to the wealth of our kingdom. A dwindling wealth, but a wealth my father clings to with every breath in his ageing body.

Thorne stands with his hands clasped behind his back, shoulders back, chin tilted. He stares at Edmund's boat as if he might be able to will it to turn around if he tries hard enough.

"Is this truly the only way?" I ask as I raise my hand and wave at the distant figure of Prince Edmund.

Edmund does not wave back.

Thorne does not answer.

Guilt swells in my stomach. I shouldn't have asked him that. Thorne cares as much for me as he does for my father's kingdom. He has faced an impossible choice, but he is doing what he believes to be right for all of us.

He is letting me go, and I vowed I would not make it harder for him than it needs to be.

I touch my elbow to his. Barely a touch, but enough so he knows I am here beside him, and that I understand.

He does not respond.

I try to smile, and keep waving.

With Thorne, I am myself – passionate, wild, free. But the clandestine moments we steal away from prying eyes feel as if they are not real sometimes.

Sometimes, when he is cold and distant in the presence of others, I wonder whether I imagine those moments. But then he whispers something to me or he looks at me with just a flicker of the passion I see in private, and I *know* I am not dreaming.

He loves me the way I love him.

But soon, I will belong to another, and the thought coils in my stomach like a serpent.

When the fanfare begins, heralding the ship's arrival at the dock, the blast of the trumpets settles deep in my gut.

In seven days' time, I will be bound to a man I have never met.

My childhood dreams of falling in love and beaming with pride on my wedding day lie in tatters. Instead, I am nothing but a pawn in a game of power I did not choose to play. And the man I love can never truly be mine.

Staring at the ship, I try to pull Edmund's features into view.

He is pale-haired, pale-skinned, and of average height. He is not smiling.

Perhaps he hates this as much as I do. For our union is not one of stolen glances and racing hearts and simmering anticipation. It was negotiated by our parents and their councillors over maps and ledgers. It is a business transaction. We are assets to be traded as our parents see fit.

Perhaps he, too, loves another who he cannot be with.

As the ship docks and the gangplank lowers with a resounding thud, sealing my fate, I draw a deep breath, readying myself to wear the mask of the dutiful princess.

Inside, I am beating my fists against the fetters of my royal cage.

But on the outside, I keep smiling. Because I know what fate awaits me if I do not.

2

EDMUND

The princess is undoubtedly beautiful. Her slender but shapely figure comes into view as the ship draws closer to the docks of Zakron. At this distance, I see nothing of the full lips and dazzling green eyes that I was promised. I do, however, see masses of loose blond hair hanging over her shoulders. The wind catches it and blows it across her face. She tucks it back, then waves at me, and her lips part into a smile. I cannot tell whether it is a true smile or a forced one. I take a moment to consider whether I care. On balance, I decide I do not.

It is her *job* to smile and look the part, so I can focus on doing what needs to be done to secure the safety and prosperity of our kingdoms.

As long as her pleasure looks convincing, that's good enough for me.

"This union is important, Edmund." My mother's dainty fingers clasp my shoulder. "But remember, it is far more important for *them* than it is for us. If we are to achieve our goals, she must be pleasing to look at, pliable, and obedient."

"You do not need to remind me, Mother. I am aware of the significance of the union, and I shall assess her accordingly."

My mother nods and smiles. "What do you think so far?" She pulls her cloak close against the chill of the wind, then hooks her arm into mine as we stare out at Zakron's docks.

Calla stands at the front of a crowd of courtiers and musicians. Flags flutter in the wind.

"She seems perfectly . . . inoffensive. From a distance." I turn to my mother and kiss her on the cheek. "Although, I must admit, I have always preferred my women with dark hair. And a little more shapely."

My mother, who herself is a brunette, rolls her eyes but smiles at my flattery. "Just remember," she says, squeezing my forearm, "if she doesn't please you, there will be others who can. Princess Calla is not the only answer to our prosperity. And if she pleases you enough to marry, but you need more for your . . . entertainment," my mother shrugs, "well, then you shall simply take a mistress."

I lace my fingers together behind my back and straighten my shoulders. I cannot be crowned king until I am wed, and five months since my father's death, I refuse to wait any longer to wear the crown. As long as Calla isn't a complete hag, I am determined to go through with this union.

My only hope is that she isn't insufferably talkative.

Quiet, pliable, and pleasing to the eye. Those are my requirements.

I have been promised by her father and his advisers that she will fill them. Soon, I will find out whether they have been telling me the truth.

∼

By the time I have disembarked from the *Desdemona*, the princess has disappeared from view, which does not fill me with optimism. Perhaps, up close, she is not as dazzling as they promised.

Thorne, the king's adviser who I've met several times on his visits to negotiate the princess's hand, approaches with an urgent stride. As usual, his dark hair is impeccably groomed. His eyes, sharp and observant, scan the surroundings before settling on me.

"My apologies, Prince Edmund." He clasps my hand and bows at the same time. "The princess was taken suddenly unwell." He chuckles and rolls his eyes. "Women and weddings. The excitement clearly became too much."

"Quite," I reply, pushing back my shoulders so the chains at my neck glint in the pale sunlight. Before I can ask *when* I might expect to meet Princess Calla, Thorne interrupts.

"Your journey was longer than we expected," he says as we begin the short walk to the waiting carriages ahead. "I was beginning to worry you had been taken by the mermaids."

I return his gesture with a nod, barely masking my distaste for his overly familiar manner. Just because we have made each other's acquaintance before does not mean he should speak to me as though we are equals. I am royalty. And soon, I will be king.

"The sea was kind," I retort. "Unfortunately, the mermaids were otherwise engaged." I clear my throat and push my hands into my pockets. "Now, tell me. Princess Calla. You assured me that she is as radiant as the morning sun. I did not discern much radiance from a distance, and now you have swept her away. Am I to assume she is a little more dull than you first implied, Thorne?"

Thorne's lips twitch. He rubs his beard with his thumb and forefinger and gives me a knowing stare. "I assure you, Your

Highness, Calla is a bright light, indeed. A little highly strung." He jerks an eyebrow. "But pleasing to the eye."

A flicker of excitement settles in my stomach. Highly strung is not ideal, but I am sure I can find a way of taming her.

"And soon," Thorne adds, "she will be all yours. To do with as you wish."

We have reached the carriages. Thorne holds open a door and ushers me inside.

"You will meet her tonight," he says, nodding as he takes a seat opposite me. "And you may hold me *personally* responsible if you do not like what you find."

3

CALLA

The banquet hall glitters with light and laughter, but I feel nothing but dread as I await the arrival of Prince Edmund. My injured arm throbs beneath the heavy brocade of my gown, even though it was tended to by my father's physician.

I tilt my head from side to side. The jewels that have been laced into my long blond braid are heavy and making my scalp ache. My neck too. Chosen to mirror the green of my eyes, they look ravishing. But I have always abhorred the price women are expected to pay for fashion.

Next to me, my mother clears her throat, indicating I should keep still and stop fidgeting.

The nobles are circling the room, their smiles bright but their eyes calculating. They know how much rides on this union. Our kingdom's power, our position in the wider world – it all depends on me playing my part tonight. It depends on me proving to Edmund that I am a bride worthy of being his queen.

"Edmund is a coveted prize," my mother reminds me as

she appears at my side. "The king's early passing surprised us all. We are lucky your father had already begun negotiations with him before he became ill. This union is a coveted one that will secure Zakron's safety for many, many years."

"Yes, we are lucky," I repeat stoically. "Edmund will be a fine king, and I should be honoured to be his queen."

My mother glares down at me. She, too, has blond hair. Although hers is now becoming a luscious shade of silver. She nods approvingly at my well-crafted response. "You're learning," she says. "You'll do us proud tonight, Calla."

At my other elbow, my father grows ever more impatient, barking at the servants to ready themselves and glancing constantly towards the doors. "Smile, daughter," he hisses through his teeth. "We must give Edmund no cause to doubt you."

I force my lips upward even as my stomach twists. I have been performing the role of dutiful daughter and perfect princess for as long as I can remember. Tonight is simply another performance. Except, much more rides on this one.

Once, a long time ago, I was the kind of girl who splashed barefoot in the sea foam dreaming of adventures. But she has been extinguished, replaced by the polished, compliant princess they demanded I become.

I used to dream of getting her back one day. Now I know the best I can hope for is that Edmund is not cruel.

At last, the herald's voice rings out. "His Royal Highness, Prince Edmund of Xandor, and Her Majesty the Queen."

Edmund and his mother appear at the far end of the hall. She has dark curly hair. It hangs loose over her shoulders, with a large pearl clip pushing it back from her ear. Her figure is full, as are her cheeks. She seems weaker than I'd imagined. More mouse-like. Not tall and strong like my mother.

I inhale deeply, clenching my skirts to stop my hands from

shaking. As Edmund strides forward, the nobles bow low before straightening to appraise my future husband. My first thought is how young he looks. He is my age – perhaps a year or two older– but he carries himself with the air of a petulant teenager.

Thorne, positioned first in line with the other nobles, watches Edmund approach. He is as adept at performing for my father as I am. Pretending he is not in love with me. Pretending he admires Edmund. Pretending he is proud that he instigated our engagement.

When Thorne greets Edmund, he dips into a low bow. Edmund stops. His mother whispers something to him, but barely acknowledges Thorne's presence. My jaw twitches with irritation. The prince knows Thorne is my father's most trusted aide, and yet he hardly deigns to look at him?

Youth and arrogance are a deadly combination in a future king, and it seems my future husband has both. In spades.

As Thorne and Edmund talk, I study the two of them. To those observing *me,* it looks as though I am staring at my future husband. But it is not Edmund I am drawn to. What my observers don't see is the turmoil beating inside my ribcage as I look at Thorne. The memories dancing across my flesh, lighting it up, and making my entire body come alive.

Memories of stolen kisses and whispered *I love you's.*

Memories I will have to vanquish if I'm to travel to Xandor and begin a new life.

"Thorne will make sure the evening goes without a hitch," my mother whispers. "Listen to him, Calla. Do as he says."

"Yes, Mother." I nod as Thorne and Edmund make their way down the line of nobles towards us.

While Thorne is dark and brooding and exudes the confidence of an experienced man, Edmund's beardless cheeks are still rounded with youth. Thorne is quick-witted, strategic, commanding. And even though I have not yet even spoken to Edmund, I can tell from his demeanour that he is none of those things. In fact, if I did not know the two of them, I would assume that Thorne was the future king. Not Edmund.

At each introduction, to our priest, our councillors, and our most accomplished academics, Edmund nods but keeps his chin raised and his posture strangely rigid. As if there is a bad smell lingering under his nose.

"As soon as we are married, Edmund will be crowned king of Xandor?" I whisper to my mother.

She tuts and keeps her eyes trained on the prince. "Yes, Calla. You know this. We have discussed it at length. He cannot be king until he is married."

Apprehension congeals in my stomach. I have not even spoken to Edmund yet, and I can clearly see what kind of king he will be.

Am I to facilitate such a man?

Am I so helpless that I must resign myself to being the catalyst for an age of ever-increasing egotism and greed? Both Edmund's and my father's?

I study the prince as he draws closer to me. How little warmth his eyes contain as they flit across the room. Despite being blue, they are dark – like the murky depths of the ocean. He assesses his surroundings. His mouth twitches. A sneer, not a smile. Clearly, he finds our hospitality lacking in grandeur.

Finally, his gaze lands on me.

I step forward in unison with my parents and drop into a deep curtsey. I cannot look at Thorne, who stands at Edmund's side and introduces us. Instead, I stare at the embroidered hem of my skirt, keeping my gaze trained towards the floor. "Your Highness," I say softly. "We are honoured to receive you, and I very much look forward to deepening our families' bonds." The platitudes I offer taste bitter on my tongue.

"The honour is mine, princess. We have long anticipated this union between our peoples." Edmund does not bow, and his speech is perfunctory. Distracted. Laced with irritation.

When I look up, I meet his eyes. I remain curtseyed, my mother too. After a few more torturous seconds, Edmund extends his hand and I take it lightly, suppressing a shiver at his icy touch.

He nods slightly and I stand, retracting my hand. I smile and wait for him to smile back. He does not, simply appraises me with a slightly disappointed frown, eyes trailing from my breasts to my hips before settling on my mouth.

I swallow hard. Bile burns in the back of my throat.

Edmund's eyes narrow, perhaps sensing my hesitation, and I curse inwardly, then quickly rearrange my features into a mask of politeness.

As we turn to greet the rest of the guests, I step in line with him and fight to maintain a calm exterior. It seems the closer I am to Edmund physically, the more I struggle to breathe.

My father takes his place at the head of the banquet table and the room descends into a quivering silence as he speaks. He introduces Edmund, sings the praises of the young prince who is about to become king, and of all the benefits our union will bring. Then he raises his glass in a toast.

All the while, Edmund stands motionless beside him. This cold, pompous prince is the man who has been chosen for me, the man to whom I must give my life. For the sake of my kingdom. But seeing him here, like this, I am beginning to wonder if he truly is the salvation my father seeks.

Is Edmund really the one who will keep us safe from the wider world? Lead us into a new and prosperous age?

Or will Prince Edmund of Xandor be the downfall of us all?

4

CALLA

Trumpets blare as the prince and I are ushered to our seats at the head of the main table. I arrange my skirts, smoothing away any wrinkles as a servant pulls out my chair. Edmund watches me coolly before taking his seat beside me.

As the first course is served, Edmund addresses me with the same detached courtesy he showed to my parents and to Thorne.

"So," he says, suppressing a yawn, "tell me, princess, what are your interests? I imagine your days are filled with feminine pursuits like embroidery and harp playing?" He speaks as if he is reading from a script.

I bristle at his assumptions but maintain an even tone. "While those activities have their place, I prefer more active pursuits. Riding, hawking, even archery on occasion." My mother would be very cross if she heard me talking about archery, but a small indignant part of me feels a sense of satisfaction as Edmund's brows rise and his eyes narrow.

He shoves a forkful of meat into his mouth and chews

loudly. "Archery? Irregular for a princess."

I bite the inside of my cheek, resisting the urge to retort. "I was fortunate to have talented tutors. Many skills are valuable for future rulers, don't you agree?"

"Hm, yes, I suppose." Edmund's tone makes it clear he does not really agree. "But you are not to *rule*." He scrapes a crust of bread around his plate, mopping up the juice from the meat. "You are a prop." He waves his hand, and a glob of juice lands on his waistcoat. "You will manage the household, provide me with heirs to the throne, and smile politely when we have visiting dignitaries. Laugh at their jokes. Flatter their egos." He meets my gaze as he bites off a chunk of bread and chews it loudly. "Is flattery a skill you possess, Princess Calla?" He leans in, his knee touching mine beneath the table. "Did your tutors teach you that?"

My hand curls into a fist beside my plate. Does he truly see me as nothing but a broodmare for his heirs and a decorative addition to his court? A whore who will ply his acquaintances with smiles and flirtations? "No, my lord, I'm afraid they did not."

Edmund reaches for my hand. He squeezes it tightly, and smiles. "Then you should find yourself a different kind of tutor. You could be a lot more" – he pauses, casting a lecherous glance at my cleavage – "*appealing*, if you put in some effort."

Slowly, I draw my hand back from his grasp, being sure to keep a smile fixed on my face. I take a sip from my glass and clear my throat. "Tell me about your kingdom, my lord. I have heard Xandor has quite wonderful beaches."

Edmund grins, then laughs loudly.

Across the room, my mother is sighing with relief. My father nods approvingly. They believe I have entertained him. They do not see what he truly is, and even if they did, they would not care.

As Edmund launches into a lengthy, self-aggrandising account of his accomplishments, completely ignoring my question about the geography of Xandor, I pick at my food, offering the occasional murmur to feign interest. He seems enthralled by the sound of his own voice, oblivious to my barely concealed disdain.

By the time the dessert course concludes, I am ready to tear out my hair. His arrogance and his disinterest in actually knowing me both confirm that our marriage will be a misery.

My only consolation is catching a glimpse of Thorne standing at the back wall, keeping watch over the festivities. When our eyes meet, he inclines his head. Just a little.

The tension in my chest eases. At least there is one person here who truly sees me.

He knows this banquet is torture for me. He can sense my spiralling despair, and with one penetrating look, he silently reminds me of the strength we draw from each other. Because I know he is finding this hard, too.

At last, Edmund's monologue ends as the final course concludes. The table is cleared, and musicians strike up a tune as dancing begins. Guests pair off and twirl across the floor.

Prince Edmund, however, makes no move to invite me for a dance. Instead, he waves over a buxom serving girl to refill his goblet. His eyes trace her curves greedily as she leans over him. When she takes his goblet, his fingers brush her wrist, teasing the bracelet that peeks out from beneath the long black sleeves of her dress.

I look away.

Thorne approaches and offers Edmund a formal bow. "Your Highness, might I have the honour of a dance with the princess? It would be a shame for her to sit idle during the revelries."

Edmund, already drunk, gestures lazily in our direction.

"Yes, yes, dance with my betrothed if you like. I'm otherwise engaged." He leers at the serving girl, who has not left his side.

"Your betrothed?" Thorne glances at me then back at Edmund. "Does this mean you have made a decision, Your Highness?"

"The decision was made before I even got here. You know that, Thorne. You made it your business to persuade me of Princess Calla's virtues before I even set eyes on her."

Thorne dips his head. "I am glad you are happy, Your Highness."

Edmund doesn't answer, just waves a dismissive hand at Thorne, then looks up at the serving girl and says, "What's your name, girl?"

"Lucielle," she replies with a giggle, smoothing her hands over her hips.

Rage burns hot inside me. How dare he make it so brazenly clear he intends to take this woman to his bed tonight? While I – his future queen – am seated beside him. And how dare *she* partake in his lechery?

As if he can sense my mood darkening, Thorne extends his hand. I take it and, as we walk to the dance floor, he squeezes my palm, grounding me.

We take our positions among the other couples. As the music swells, Thorne pulls me close, one hand warm at my back. Our bodies sway in effortless sync, our hearts beating as one.

For a blissful moment, all else fades, leaving only this: the music, the movement, Thorne's touch. Here, I do not have to play a role or bend myself to fit another's ideals. Here, with him, I can simply be.

We do not speak as we dance, just hold each other. It is over too quickly. As we draw apart, Thorne's fingers trail lightly down my arm, a secret caress amid the distraction of the crowd. "Have courage," he whispers near my ear. "You are stronger than anyone knows. But *I* know you, Calla. I know how brave you are. You should be so proud of what you're doing for your people."

Thorne's words of encouragement make my throat tighten with emotion. I squeeze his hand and stare desperately into his eyes. "What if I can't go through with it? What if I get to the altar and I can't bring myself to bind myself to that man for the rest of my life?" I whisper, finally saying the words I've kept locked in my throat for so long. "Edmund is arrogant, cold . . . nothing like the man I hoped to wed." I pause, inhaling deeply. "Nothing like *you.*"

Thorne's grip on my hand tightens, at first soothingly, then almost painfully. His eyes flash with something I cannot read.

"You know it hurts me when you talk like that," he says. "You know it causes guilt to wrap itself around my useless heart and squeeze until I can barely breathe." He presses one hand to his chest while the other keeps hold of me.

"I'm sorry." I try to keep smiling, but the facade is fading. "I know this is just as hard for you as it is for me. It's just . . . is this really the only way?" This time, my smile changes. It becomes real as I whisper, "Could we not run away together, my love? Run away from here and live a simple life? Just the two of us." I search his eyes. "I have loved you for as long as I can remember. There has never been another man who even came close to stealing my heart. Only you."

Thorne presses his lips together – as if he is struggling to keep his very soul inside his body – then lets go of me and turns to walk away from the dance floor, hand resting on the small of my back as he guides me slowly back towards Edmund.

"We must not lose our resolve now, Calla," he says firmly through gritted teeth. "We have worked too hard to secure this alliance through your marriage. We all must make sacrifices for the good of the kingdom. We must think of the greater good, not our own foolish desires."

He stares at Edmund, who is now openly groping Lucielle's backside. Then his demeanour softens, and he turns to smile at me. It is a smile that disarms me every time. "It's not only a king who can find *distractions* outside of marriage." His thumb rubs gently against the silk of my gown. The smallest circles. Circles no one would ever see but which send waves of heat up the curve of my spine.

"If you wish, I will travel with you to your new home. All you need to do is request that I am on your staff."

"Travel with me?"

Thorne presses closer.

"We can be just as we are now. Edmund will not know or care." Thorne jerks his head towards Lucielle. "Perhaps you should bring her, too. She seems only too happy to amuse him."

I recoil inwardly at the thought of such a thing, even though I know it is the way things have been done for centuries. Kings and queens, wives and husbands, play-acting at marriage while having torrid affairs.

Thorne continues speaking in a low, gravelly voice. "I will be yours, Calla, even if you can never truly be mine. That is the price I am willing to pay for the sake of our kingdom's survival. What price can you offer?"

He stops walking, turns to me, and holds my gaze for a long, lingering moment. Before I can answer, he bows, then turns away and strides over to my father. Thorne says something and my father laughs loudly, holding his rotund stomach while he claps Thorne on the shoulder.

I inhale deeply and flex my fingers at my sides. If Thorne can resign himself to watching another man by my side for the rest of our lives in order to protect our people, then surely I cannot protest my part in things?

I dislike Edmund, but I'd trust Thorne with my life. If he truly believes this is the best path, then I should too. I know that, and yet as I return to Edmund, my stomach remains twisted in vicious knots of dread.

When I take my place beside him, Edmund doesn't even look at me. He just yawns, then stands up. His chair scrapes the floor. He searches for Lucielle, who is now standing with the other servers at the back of the hall, and nods at her.

He does not say goodbye or goodnight to me, simply staggers out of the banquet hall with Lucielle a few unsubtle paces behind him.

I look down at my hands, biting back tears. What price am I willing to pay to ensure our kingdom's survival? Am I willing to barter my soul for such an abstract concept?

I am twisting my fingers in my lap when a shadow falls over me and I look up to find my mother. "This is the way of things," she says bluntly. "Edmund will have his fun. But you will be his wife."

"What does that mean? *Wife*?" I ask defiantly.

My mother has always been more tolerant of my outspokenness than my father. She hesitates for a moment, then sighs heavily. For the first time in a long time, I see a shimmer of sympathy in her expression. "It means . . . do your duty, Calla." She nods firmly, then glances over to where my father is shamelessly flirting with Edmund's mother, Queen Katherine. A small sigh shakes her chest. "It means do your duty, do not ask questions, and do not make the mistake of thinking you are owed happiness in this life. None of us are. Especially women, and especially princesses."

5

CALLA

Pale morning light streams in through the open shutters. My chambers are cool, but the texture of the air tells me it will become warmer as the sun climbs higher in the sky.

I free my hair from its braid and shake so it falls loosely over my shoulders.

"My lady, your hair becomes glossier and stronger every day." My chambermaid Helene brushes it aside so she can lace the back of my gown.

"It is a shame the rest of me does not share that same character trait," I mutter.

Helene laughs. She has a soft, bubbly laugh that reminds me of my old nursemaid.

I clear my throat and press my palms to my stomach. "Helene," I say hesitantly, "did you happen to see what became of Prince Edmund after he left the banquet last night? I believe he was with the kitchen girl, Lucielle."

Helene's hands still on the laces. I turn to find her gazing at the floor, clearly reluctant to reply. I shouldn't have asked. I do not need to know the answer. And yet, I do.

"Please, I would like to know the truth," I prod gently.

Helene sighs, then meets my eyes. She tucks a strand of greying hair behind her ear. "Yes, my lady. The prince was heard in his chambers with her until the early hours." She presses her lips together and, though her features show no sign of displeasure, her eyes have darkened.

My stomach drops. Edmund truly did ignore all decorum and propriety to bed a servant on the night of our formal betrothal.

"Do not think ill of Lucielle, though, my lady. She is only young. Your age, in fact. It is easy to be swayed by a prince's charms."

I feel ill. Is this to be my life? Bound to a man who craves only his own pleasure, who views me as an object for trading purposes? I rush to the window and throw it open, gulping fresh air. Waves crash on the distant cliffs, gulls call from high above. I grip the windowsill and my knuckles whiten.

"My lady?" Helene approaches tentatively, resting a gentle hand on my elbow. "Perhaps you should speak with the king about Prince Edmund."

I start to shake my head, then pause. Helene has been my confidant for years. If she advises me to talk to my father, perhaps I should listen.

"You have been against the match from the very beginning of this enterprise," Helene tuts. "But have you ever told your parents how you feel about it?"

"My parents care little for what I feel," I reply.

Helene smiles sadly, her hazel eyes deep and full of pity.

"You really think my father would reconsider the match?" I ask hesitantly.

Helene gestures for me to sit down and begins to brush my

hair with long, soothing strokes. "I cannot say, but you are his only daughter. If you speak from your heart, he may yet be swayed. More importantly, though, princess . . . Could you live with yourself knowing you didn't *try* to speak up for yourself?"

A spark of hope flickers in my chest. It is foolish, and I know my father well enough to know I am setting myself up for disappointment by even entertaining the notion he might take pity on me. But I also know that I have never done anything brave or courageous in my life.

And if I'm to spend the rest of it in shackles, I should at least like to be able to say I stood up for myself.

Just once.

Taking a deep breath, I turn and squeeze Helene's hands. "You're right. I must at least try."

She smiles encouragingly. "I know your father can be stubborn, but he does love you. In his own way. Make him understand why this marriage troubles you so. Not just for the kingdom but for you." She taps my chest – the place above my heart.

I inhale slowly and deeply, pushing my shoulders back and trying to replicate the way Thorne looks when he strides into a room. Confident. Assertive.

Buoyed by her words, I exit my chambers with fresh resolve. My father may still insist on the alliance, but I will lay my doubts before him and at least be able to look myself in the eye and know I did my best to stop it.

My courage rising, I hurry to my father's study. Helene overestimates my father's affection for me. She is sweet, and kind, and wants to see the best in everyone she meets.

Deep down, I know my father does not care whether the match benefits *me*. But I have to believe that, deep down, he still cares for our people – who deserve a just and honourable king. Not a smarmy snake like Edmund.

~

I stand outside my father's study and take a deep breath to gather my courage. My palms grow damp as I knock on the heavy wooden door. At my father's bark of "Enter," I slip inside.

He sits behind a massive desk, scribbling on parchment, and doesn't look up as I approach. "What is it, daughter?"

"Father, I've come to talk to you about Prince Edmund." My voice wavers only slightly. I exhale through a tightened jaw.

At this, his quill stills. My father lifts his shaggy head to fix me with an icy stare. "Oh? And what about the prince?"

I lift my chin. "Edmund's behaviour last night reveals his unworthiness to rule, both over me and our kingdom. He is arrogant, rude, and cares nothing for propriety. He disrespected me and, by extension, you and our people. I do not believe this match bodes well for —"

My father blinks slowly. Colour rises in his cheeks, and he slams his fist on the desk, making me jump. "You dare question this alliance?" he roars.

I shrink back, the volume of his anger rattling the marrow deep in my bones. "Father, please, if you would just listen —"

He surges to his feet, face mottled with rage. "Do you understand nothing, foolish girl? This marriage is essential for our kingdom's future!"

Spittle flies as he rants about the trade benefits, military protection, everything the union will bring. I open my mouth to protest again, but he slashes the air with his hand.

"Not another word! The match is set. You will marry Prince Edmund one week from today." His eyes flash dangerously. "Do you hear me, daughter?"

My rebuttals die in my throat. The courage that bloomed in

my stomach wilts and withers. I bow my head. "Of course, father. Forgive my hesitation."

He harrumphs, settling back into his chair. "I don't want to hear any more from you. In fact, I would prefer not to see you at all until the wedding day."

Blinking back tears, I turn and walk slowly from the study. Even though my legs are shaking. Like it or not, in one week I will become Edmund's wife and queen.

One week.

I round a corner and, in my daze-like state, crash straight into a pair of familiar arms. "Calla?" Thorne braces his hands on my shoulders and holds me steady. I only realise I am crying when he wipes a tear from my cheek.

"I begged my father to reconsider. He refused." I shake my head. A few strands of hair have escaped my braid and fall over my face. "I'm sorry. It's not that I don't trust you. I know the marriage is what Zakron needs. I just can't bear it." I bury my face in my hands. "I can't bear the thought of it, Thorne."

Thorne tucks my hair behind my ear, then tilts my face up to look at him.

I stand on tiptoes and bring my lips towards his, but he stops me abruptly. Looking up and down the empty corridor, he takes my hand, then jerks me into a nearby alcove.

In the shadows, he holds me close and this time kisses me deeply. It is a searching kiss that makes my entire body melt into him. With one hand on the back of my neck, he trails his lips down my throat.

I lean back against the cold stone wall and comb my fingers through his hair, encouraging his lips lower as my nipples peak beneath his touch.

"Calla," he whispers, hands settling on my waist, "you don't need to worry. Take me with you, and I will always be here." Firmly, he spins me around and, one at a time, places my hands on the wall, palms flat. "Always here to make you feel the way a queen should feel." He slips his hand beneath my skirt and his fingers dance up the inside of my thigh.

I reach for his wrist to stop him, but he grabs my hand and returns it to the wall. Lips teasing the spot beneath my ear, he whispers, "Keep still, my queen," then he parts my legs a little further and trails a long, slow finger through my waiting folds.

As heat floods to my core, his expert fingers coax moans and sighs from my body. He slips his hand over my mouth, and tells me to stay quiet. But the electricity zipping up my spine makes me want to scream his name again and again and again.

My hands become fists, punching the wall as I try to hold back the sounds that would reveal us to the world.

"Come for me, Calla," he whispers. "I love feeling you come when I have my fingers inside you."

I push back against him. He wraps an arm around my waist and holds me tight. My hands find my breasts, and his mouth finds my neck, and when my orgasm washes over me, he lets me shudder and fall back into him.

Breathless and shaking, I whisper, "I love you," as my body begins its descent back to earth.

Thorne spins me back around, cups my face in his hands, and kisses my forehead. "I love you too, Calla." He stares into my eyes.

My cheeks are flushed, my legs trembling, my heart aching.

"I can protect you from Edmund's stupidity and his indifference, Calla. Take me with you and let us do *this* for the rest of our lives." Before I can answer, he reaches into his pocket. Something glints in the dim light of our hiding place. "I cannot give you a ring," he says. "But I can give you this as a symbol of my love."

I look down. He holds a delicate gold bracelet in his palm. He turns it over. "It is inscribed, you see," he says.

I squint in the darkness and I read the inscription aloud. *"Eternal in secret, bound by the stars – forever yours, unseen but felt. T."*

Tears bite at the back of my throat. Hot and sharp. But they are happy tears this time. I hold out my wrist and Thorne fastens the bracelet around it.

"I will never take it off," I promise him.

He lifts my hand and kisses my knuckles. "And I will never leave your side," he whispers.

6

CALLA

Like a doll in a music box, I stand on top of a low pedestal in my private chambers as the royal seamstress makes alterations to my wedding gown. The room is bathed in late morning sunlight. It streams through the towering arched windows and casts long shadows across the stone floor.

The curtains billow gently, the ocean breeze beckoning salty air into the room. I close my eyes and tilt my face towards the sun, but the seamstress tugs my skirt and tells me to keep still.

Then she clicks her fingers and asks Helene to close the window. "It is blowing the fabric," the seamstress mutters.

"The gown is beautiful, my lady." Helene hooks the window closed and smiles at me when she turns around. "Truly beautiful. Prince Edmund is a lucky man."

I try to smile back, but my throat constricts. I cough to clear it, earning myself another disgruntled sigh from the seamstress and a sympathetic hand-pat from Helene.

My gaze falls to the intricate details of the dress my mother chose. The corseted bodice is crafted from rich ivory silk brocade, hand embroidered with pearls and silver thread. The full skirt blooms out in layers of the softest silk, cut to flow gracefully with my every move. Delicate lace sleeves kiss my shoulders, while the low scooped neckline is trimmed in more pearls. The veil is almost as long as the train. It is a gown fit for a queen. It is truly stunning.

I hate every inch of it.

I wince as a pin pricks my skin.

"Apologies, Your Highness," the seamstress murmurs around her mouthful of pins. I nod and raise my arms again, staring at my reflection in the full-length mirror.

The gown itself is undoubtedly stunning, but seeing myself in it makes my stomach churn with anxiety. In seven days' time, I will walk down the aisle in this dress and bind myself irrevocably to Prince Edmund.

After a few more adjustments, the seamstress gathers her supplies. "I believe it is finished for now, princess. I will return to make final adjustments the day before the wedding." With a curtsy, she bustles out.

I step down from the pedestal and turn to see Helene watching me closely. "You look radiant, my lady," she offers kindly, although the sentiment of her words is not reflected in her smile or her gaze.

"Do I?" I say with a bitter laugh. "I feel like a sacrificial lamb being trussed up for slaughter."

Helene clasps my hand in sympathy. "Everything will be all right," she says, moving to my back to help me shrug out of the dress. "I'm sorry I told you to go to your father. I honestly thought..."

I shake my head and rub Helene's hand. "Please, don't apologise. I am glad I spoke my mind."

As Helene hangs up the dress, I stride over to the window and stare out at the ocean.

Prince Edmund's ship waits in the docks. Her sails are visible, but she is still. Waiting to carry me away to a land I have never visited. I tuck my hair behind my ear, and my bracelet catches my eye. I run my fingers over it, and close my eyes.

Instead of picturing myself alone on the bow of the ship, waving beside a stony-faced Prince Edmund, I imagine Thorne standing behind us. I imagine his presence soothing me. I picture days spent together in my new palace when Edmund is travelling or visiting the whores he will inevitably take to his bed.

"Perhaps it won't be as bad as I thought," I whisper.

"My lady?" Helene is at my elbow, holding my robe. As she helps me put it on, her eyes flick to my wrist. "My lady, what a beautiful bracelet. Where did you get it? I have not seen it in your collection."

I hesitate, bothering the bracelet, twisting it round and round. "It was a gift." I meet her eyes, and my lips curl into a smile. For two years, I have kept my love for Thorne secret. Even from Helene, who I trust more than any other.

"My lady?" Helene frowns. "Was it from the prince?"

I shake my head. Thorne swore me to secrecy. But Helene can be trusted, and if she is to come with us to Xandor, it could only be beneficial to have her as an ally in our love affair. "It is from Thorne."

Helene's eyes widen. Her mouth falls open but then she closes it again and folds her arms in front of her stomach. "Truly? Thorne?"

I nod, then remove the bracelet and show her the inscription.

"Then you and he . . .?"

"Yes," I confess. "It began a long time ago. He loves me, and

I love him, and he has vowed to come with me to Xandor. He will transfer to Edmund's staff and protect me. Love me." I take the bracelet back, and gesture for Helene to fix it back on my wrist. "He will be my husband in all but name, and *this* is how I will survive Edmund."

"But Thorne arranged the marriage," Helene mutters.

"Because he cares deeply for our kingdom." I sigh and look down at my wrist. "And he is making a great sacrifice for our people."

Helene's expression is unreadable. She helps me fasten the bracelet, then curls her fingers around my forearm. "Princess, you plan to continue the affair even after you are wed?"

"I do."

She sits down on the concrete sill below the window. She frowns deeply at my words. "Are you certain that is wise?"

I bristle, pulling my robe tightly around my waist. "You yourself said I should speak the truth. Do not punish me for being honest with you, Helene."

"I am not punishing you, my lady. I am simply concerned for your safety. Xandor has been known to execute queens who have –"

"I do not need words of caution, Helene," I snap, bracing my hands on my hips, elbows jutting out.

"Of course, Your Highness," Helene says gently. "I only mean . . . are you sure Thorne is trustworthy? Is his affection sincere?"

"I am more sure of him than of anything else in this world." I meet her gaze and hold it steady.

Helene dips her head. "Then forgive me, princess. It is not my place to question your choices. I only want you to be happy and safe." With a final, sad smile, she stands and embraces me. "Your secret is safe with me."

7

THORNE

King Magnus leads the way as we ride out from the castle, his great bulk nearly swallowing the poor horse beneath him. At his side is Prince Edmund, who looks bored and irritated to be included in this hunting excursion. Also pathetically unsteady on a horse.

I remain at the rear of the hunting party, eyes sharp, taking in the surrounding woods. Out here, away from the confines of court and prying ears, tongues often loosen. I attribute my current standing in Magnus's court to my ability to quietly fade into the background in such situations. To listen and learn.

"How are you finding our hospitality, Prince Edmund?" Magnus bellows.

Edmund sniffs. "It is rather . . . rustic."

The king chuckles, apparently missing the insult. "Soon our kingdoms shall be united." He pauses, then raises his eyebrows. "I hope you've found the princess to your liking."

At this, Edmund smirks, and I force myself not to react. Let him boast and preen. Calla is but a means to an end.

"She's an exquisite prize, to be sure," Edmund replies crassly. "I look forward to taming that fiery spirit."

"I hope she hasn't been too outspoken," Magnus tuts. "I gave her a talking-to this morning, but if you need me to be more firm –"

Edmund shakes his head and laughs. "I will let you know after our next meeting. When shall I see her again?" He glances at his nails, scraping free some dirt from beneath them.

King Magnus clicks his fingers. "Thorne, when is Prince Edmund to see my daughter again?"

I incline my head demurely, pretending to defer to his superiority. Trotting closer to Edmund, I reply, "You will meet with Princess Calla again tomorrow, Your Highness. I'm afraid today she is preoccupied with preparations for your nuptials."

Edmund simply nods at me, then turns back to the king. As they begin to reminisce about Edmund's late father, I suck air past my teeth and hold it in my throat. I seethe at their pomposity.

How infallible they think they are. How righteous. How divine.

They believe they know everything, see everything. They would not even entertain the idea that they could be plucked from their thrones and cast aside like yesterday's scraps.

They have no idea what I have sacrificed in order to find a way into their inner circle. That while they drink and whore and boast, I plot to overthrow their decadence.

Fools.

Their status and crowns cannot touch the power I will soon wield. The power Calla will help me steal from their cold, dead fingers.

8

CALLA

My father insists Edmund and I spend some quality time together to get better acquainted. Through gritted teeth, I agree. Even though it is not a question but an order.

I slept poorly last night.

Helene's reaction to my confession played over and over in my mind. Something about her words bothered me. "Are you sure Thorne is trustworthy?"

I answered yes without truly thinking about my reply. But last night, as the moon rose high in the sky and I paced the cold stone floor of my chamber, I could not help reeling through my memories of our time together.

I have always trusted him. Implicitly.

I have never questioned his words or his motives.

But does Helene know something I don't? Is that why she questioned our union? As part of our staff, she sees things I don't. Hears whispers I don't. What if she knows of something that would call Thorne's character into question? She has always wanted the best for me, looked after me more than even my own mother has. Should I not investigate her questions further?

I shake my head and try to pay attention to what Edmund is saying. He looks equally displeased as we stroll stiffly through the castle gardens together.

"A pleasant day," he remarks with an insincere smile. "Though I could use a little more conversation on your part."

"Of course. My apologies."

Edmund plucks a rose, sniffs it disdainfully, and tosses it aside. "Do you have nothing you wish to ask me?" he says, raising an eyebrow. "Nothing you'd like to know about your future husband?" He edges closer and his hand finds my waist.

I pull back and keep walking. "I'm sure we will have plenty of time to get to know one another once we are situated in Xandor."

Edmund sighs grumpily and shoves his hands into his pockets.

A cool breeze sweeps through the rose garden. I look up and point to the grey clouds that seem to have gathered almost instantaneously above us. "We should return to the castle. A storm comes."

Dismissively, Edmund waves his hand. "It will pass. The sea breeze will blow the clouds away before the rain starts."

"I do not believe so, my lord –" I'm about to explain my reasoning when a crack of thunder cuts through my words. Fat raindrops begin pelting down. Edmund protests loudly, holds his hands above his head – as if this might protect him – then turns and runs towards the summerhouse. He does not take my hand or offer me any assistance, just runs.

I follow, picking my skirts up and trying in vain to stop the deluge ruining my carefully braided hair. I trip as I step up into the summerhouse. Still, Edmund does not help me.

He stands in the corner, sulking and shaking water from

his velvet doublet. "Well, this is simply perfect. I'm soaked through!"

I bite my tongue to refrain from snapping back. Sheltering beneath the domed roof, I wring water from my skirts, breathing deeply to remain civil.

"I'm not leaving until the rain stops," Edmund snaps.

"A wise idea, my lord," I reply deferentially, even though I'm seething on the inside.

Edmund narrows his eyes at me, then sits down. He pats the space next to him on the bench, but I ignore him and remain standing. I clear my throat, casting about for a conversational topic. "I was sorry to hear about your father passing. You must miss him terribly."

A cloud passes over Edmund's face. He looks out at the rain, shoulders slumping slightly. He does not reply.

Seeing his unguarded grief, I feel a flicker of sympathy. "I cannot imagine suddenly losing my father and having the weight of the kingdom thrust upon me."

Edmund nods, glancing down. He picks at a loose thread in his doublet. "There are days I wish . . ." He stops himself, shaking his head. But I can read the rest in his eyes. Days he wishes his father was still alive.

"It's all right, you know," I say gently. "To grieve, and admit this is difficult. It does not make you any less fit to lead."

Edmund searches my face. His expression has changed. He looks older all of a sudden. More like a real person instead of a caricature of a terrible prince. "You're rather wise, aren't you?" The corner of his mouth quirks upwards. He reaches for my hand.

Something tells me to offer it to him.

I laugh softly. "So I've been told. Usually when voicing opinions my tutors did not share."

Edmund traces his index finger across my palm. My

instinct is to pull away, but something in his face makes me pause.

"Edmund," I say softly, "it's all right if you don't *want* to lead yet. You know we can postpone the wedding. It does not have to –"

His finger stops. His light touch becomes harder, and his fingernail makes a crescent-shaped dent in my skin. I try to take back my hand, but he holds me tightly. He looks up at me, then stands, gripping my upper arms and pushing me into the corner of the summerhouse. "You calculating little whore," he spits. "You would use my father's death, my grief, to your own ends? To manipulate me into postponing the marriage?" He shoves me and I hit my head on the wooden panel behind me.

"I swear to you, my lord, that was not my intention. My concern for you was sincere. I thought I sensed some reluctance on your part, and I was simply suggesting that if we worked together –"

Edmund bunches his fist and punches the wall beside my head. His eyes are dark, and he is breathing fast.

I duck out from beneath him and stumble down the steps back into the rain. Then I run as fast as I can back to the castle.

It is the middle of the afternoon, so I have no idea whether Thorne will be in his chambers, and I know with certainty that I should not be here. But I cannot be anywhere else.

I need him.

I pound hard on his door with clenched fists. I call his name. I don't care who hears me.

After barely a minute, the door clatters open and he jerks me inside.

"Calla, what in the name of the gods are you doing? You

could have been seen." He stops, his anger fading as he takes in my bedraggled appearance.

"I'm sorry," I whisper. "I'm so sorry."

"What happened?" He rests his hands on my shoulders and looks into my eyes. "Is it Edmund?"

I shake my head, unable to put into words what just happened, and fold myself into Thorne's arms. Tucking my head under his chin, I listen to his heart beating steadily in his chest and try to calm my own breathing to meet his. When I finally explain what happened, I do not look at him for fear of the disappointment I might see in his eyes. "I'm afraid he'll go to my father. What if I made him so angry he intends to call off the wedding?"

"I thought that was what you wanted," Thorne spits, letting me go and turning away from me. I have never seen him angry with me before, and the sudden souring of his tone makes me wince.

"I did, but not like this." Tears bite at my throat. "I thought Edmund was having doubts. I thought I'd found a way out. I thought there might be a way to appeal to his kinder side. To unite our kingdoms without my needing to marry him. But all I did was make him angry."

Thorne braces his hands on the top of the fireplace. Flames crackle in the grate. He shakes his head. "You silly, silly, girl. What have you done?"

I walk over to him and rest my palm on his shoulder. "I can fix it," I whisper. "Tell me how to fix it, my love."

With a sigh, Thorne turns to face me. He looks me up and down, and his eyes flicker. I am suddenly aware that my wet clothes are clinging to my skin. He closes the gap between us and grasps my waist with both hands. "Do you truly wish to know how to repair the damage you've done?" he asks, pressing his forehead to mine.

I nod as Thorne's fingers trace the bracelet on my wrist.

"You must show Edmund what he can expect when he takes you to his bed."

My entire body tenses. I pull back a little and look into Thorne's eyes. "You mean . . .?"

He nods slowly. "Give him a promise of what's to come. Persuade him you are sorry. Make him forget what happened today."

"You are asking me to go to his bed?" I shake my head and pace over to the window. "How could you ask that of me? How could you *want* that of me? When we have never . . .?"

I sense Thorne moving closer. This time, he doesn't touch me. Instead, he gently frees my hair from its braid and teases it until it is hanging loose over my shoulders. Then he sweeps it away from my neck and leans closer, his lips tantalisingly close to my ear. "The thought of you with him drives me wild with jealousy," he mutters, pressing closer. "It makes me want to tear his limbs from his pale, useless body. It makes me want to slit his throat and push his corpse into the ocean."

I close my eyes as he traces his fingers down the side of my neck and across my collar bone.

"But we have come too far, sacrificed too much, to let it all go to waste."

"Maybe it wouldn't be a waste. Maybe it would allow us to be together," I whisper.

Thorne's hands slide down to my breasts and beneath the neckline of my dress. "Perhaps it would have," he says quietly, finding my nipple and pinching it between his fingers. "But do you really think no one heard you shouting outside my chambers, Calla?"

He pinches a little harder and makes me gasp with the heady mixture of pleasure and pain.

"It wouldn't take much for someone to put two and two

together and tell the king. First, you rejected Edmund and tried to persuade him to cancel the wedding. Then you came running to me." He stops, takes his hands away, then starts to unlace the back of my dress. "Your father would have me killed." He kisses the bare flesh between my shoulder blades. "And you would be locked in the tower for the rest of your life." He sighs and presses his cheek to my back as he lowers my dress down over my breasts. "I cannot stand the thought of you being with another man, but I would rather that than have you spend the rest of your days in chains."

A violent shiver zips down my spine, and I can't tell whether it is because of Thorne's words, or the cold, or the way he is peeling my dress from my body.

"Edmund cannot be my first." I spin in his arms as the dress falls to the floor, exposing my body to Thorne in a way it has never been exposed before.

He stands back and looks at me. He scrapes his fingers through his hair and shakes his head. "Calla, you are so beautiful."

I close the gap between us.

He cups my face with his hands and kisses me softly. "Lie with me tonight, Calla. Let me be the first man to truly know you." He kisses me again, and my body lights up as his hands begin to roam my back.

I clasp my hands together behind his neck and stare into his dark, intoxicating gaze. "I want that," I whisper. "I want you."

Thorne kisses me again, then he sweeps me into his arms and carries me to his bed.

As Thorne gently lays me down on the soft silk sheets, I feel as if my entire world has shifted. This is not the first time we have been alone together, but it is the first time we have allowed ourselves to go this far. The room is lit by the dancing shadows of the fire, and I can see the flicker of determination in Thorne's eyes as he removes his clothes, then lowers himself onto me.

I kiss him deeply, tracing the contours of his chest and his back.

He brushes my lips with his thumb, then lowers his mouth to my breasts and uses his tongue to tease moans from my lips.

Moving down my body, he kisses my stomach, the sensitive skin behind my knees, the inside of my thighs. I shiver as his tongue finds my core, and grip the bedsheets when he looks up from between my legs. His eyes meet mine and he grins.

"Come here." I beckon for him to sit up, then lower my mouth onto him and sigh as he groans for me.

For a moment, his hands rest on the back of my head, but then he pushes me gently back onto the pillows. My body tingles with anticipation. He kisses me again, deeply and passionately, arching over me.

I can feel him at my entrance – hard and ready for me – but he stays there a moment, staring into my eyes. "You're certain?" he asks, stroking my face.

I nod and hook my legs around his waist, pulling him closer.

As he slides inside me, I gasp and my back arches, toes curling. He waits, lacing his fingers with mine and holding my hand tightly. "Tell me when you're ready," he whispers.

Slowly, my body adjusts to his possession. I nod. A gasp escapes my lips, a mixture of shock and pleasure, as he starts to move slowly inside me.

Thorne's eyes are fierce, hungry, and filled with a raw desire that I've never seen before. I moan softly, kissing him as he begins to move. As I start to move my hips, he picks up the pace, thrusting deeper and harder, his rhythm matching my own.

With each movement, a shockwave courses through my body.

Thorne's hands are everywhere, caressing me, holding me close. I cling to him, scraping my nails down his back, then slipping my hand between us to tease my throbbing clit while he fucks me.

I close my eyes and surrender to the sensations that are taking me over, crying out his name as he takes me higher and higher. My body trembles as Thorne continues to move inside me.

When the inevitable surge of release begins to build, a wave of pure ecstasy threatening to consume me, I bring his lips to mine and kiss him again. I hold him there as waves of pleasure ripple through my body. Thorne's own release follows soon after, his body shuddering as he quietly groans my name.

Breathless, I stroke his face. He presses his forehead to mine, then his fingers find the bracelet on my wrist. "Never forget how much I love you, Calla," he whispers. "Promise me you'll never forget."

I bring his hand to my lips and kiss his knuckles. "I promise."

9

CALLA

I wake in Thorne's arms. His body is warm. Soft and strong at the same time. I sigh and wriggle back against him, but he kisses my shoulder and tells me we should rise.

"The sun is setting. You should go and find Edmund."

A knot of panic forms instantly in my stomach. I had forgotten my promise to seduce the prince.

"I don't like the thought of another man touching me," I whisper. "Especially tonight. So soon after we –"

"Imagine you are with me," Thorne mutters, nibbling my earlobe. "Think of me, and imagine it is my lips you're kissing. My body moving against yours."

Then he is gone. Standing up, he grabs his robe from the bedpost and shrugs himself into it. He pours himself a glass of wine from the jug on his desk, then pours one for me.

After I have dressed again, he offers it to me, and I drink it down quickly.

I move to the mirror and begin to try and re-braid my hair,

but Thorne shakes his head at me. "Leave it loose," he says firmly. "Trust me, Calla. Leave it loose."

I pause, studying my reflection. There are no marks on my body, but I can still feel Thorne's touch. His lips. The sparks he coaxed from me.

"You should change first." He nods at my crumpled and still-damp dress. "Don't let anyone see you leaving here, though." He takes my elbow and walks me to the door. "If they see you, tell them you were stuck in the storm."

"I was," I reply as he pulls open the door.

"Precisely. Good girl." He kisses me swiftly, looks up and down the corridor, then nudges me out. "Come and find me tomorrow. Not tonight. It's too dangerous."

"Thorne . . ."

"Go, quickly." He smiles at me. A proud smile. "You can do this. I have faith in you."

And then the door closes, and I'm alone.

I stand for a long moment, on the verge of begging him to let me back in and tell me one more time why this is necessary. But then I hear footsteps in the distance, and I know I must hurry.

When I reach my chambers, Helene is stoking the fire and turns to greet me with a broad smile. Her smile drops when she sees my wet clothes. "Princess," she tuts. "You know better than to get caught in the rain."

"It began very quickly," I mutter as Helene helps me out of my clothes and into a robe.

"Well, yes, but you're usually so good at predicting the storms," Helene says, rubbing my shoulders as I visibly shiver. "I'll make you some tea." She ushers me into an armchair by the fire and offers me a blanket. "Get you warmed up."

"I need to go and speak to Edmund." I pause, then add,

"Make sure he got back all right. We were separated when the rain started."

Helene's forehead creases into a frown, but she simply nods at me. "After you're warmed up," she says sternly. "That's an order."

~

I wake in darkness. The fire crackles quietly in the grate as I peel open my tired eyes. Next to me, there is a cold mug of herbal tea.

I fell asleep.

I fell asleep!

After all I promised Thorne . . . how could I have let this happen?

I jump to my feet, pull on my nightdress, and slip a cloak over the top of it. I know Edmund resides in the quarters in the East Wing. And I am certain I can persuade his guards to let me past. I creep through the silent halls, my feet cold as ice on the chilled flagstone floor.

To reach the East Wing, I must take the stairs opposite Thorne's quarters.

I am on the bottom step when I hear something behind me.

I turn and, from the shadow of the stairwell, see his door slowly opening. My heart swells in my chest. A smile flutters on my lips. But something about his demeanour stops me from revealing myself.

He hesitates, glancing each way down the corridor. Then he exits and hurries in the opposite direction.

My breath catches. I look up the spiral stairs towards Edmund's chambers. I glance back at Thorne's disappearing silhouette. His bracelet is cool on my skin. Something propels me to follow him.

Quietly, I creep through the castle, following Thorne out into the courtyard that houses my father's favourite fountain. As he steps into the moonlight, I remain in the shadows.

The courtyard is completely walled in. Thorne pauses in front of the fountain. He glances around, then whistles softly.

Moments later a cloaked figure detaches itself from the darkness and joins him. I creep as close as I dare, sticking to the shadows, holding my breath for fear of being discovered.

"What news?" A woman's voice.

Thorne shakes his head, then chuckles. "A close call, but I persuaded our princess to use her best assets to keep Edmund on side."

The woman chuckles too, then tips back the hood of her cloak, exposing long dark curls and big eyes. Hungrily, Thorne pulls her to him and kisses her.

He kisses her.

I know that woman.

I have seen her before.

His lips meet hers, and his hands roam her body. It is as if he is ravenous and she is the only thing that can satiate his hunger. Without a word, he hooks his hands beneath her and lifts her onto the rim of the fountain. He positions himself between her legs. She fumbles for his belt. Then she tips back her head and stifles a cry as he enters her.

Nausea rises in my throat. Hot and urgent.

Lucielle? The serving girl who went to Edmund's bed?

I slam my hand over my mouth to stop myself from shouting or vomitting or both. I stumble back and brace myself against the wall. I can't look away.

When they are done, she hops down and rearranges her skirt. Smooths it. Grins playfully at him. "I cannot wait to be your queen," she says, kissing his cheek.

"And I cannot wait to have you beside me when I take the

throne from Edmund and throw Calla in the dungeon," Thorne breathes, biting her lower lip and squeezing her hip.

"Can I watch?" she asks. "When you tell her you were simply using her all this time? Can I be there to see the look on her poor, sad little face?"

Thorne's voice dips into a low, gravelly timbre. "I wouldn't have it any other way."

The woman bobs gleefully up and down on the soles of her feet.

"You know, I sent her to Edmund's bed." Thorne chuckles and fastens his belt.

Lucielle lets out a loud cackle. "Oh, the poor lamb." She looks Thorne up and down. "Edmund is certainly nowhere *near* the man you are, Thorne."

He grins at her and snatches another kiss.

When she stands back, she taps her wrist. "Did you find my bracelet?" she asks, tilting her head. "I'm certain I left it in your chambers."

I look down. Suddenly, the bracelet feels as if it is burning my skin. I turn around, fumbling quietly for the door and fall through it. I make too much noise, and I'm certain I hear them clamouring to run after me but I don't stop.

Somehow, I make it back to my chambers before bending over and releasing the contents of my stomach onto the floor.

I am still vomiting when Helene appears at my side. I can't hear what she's saying, but I know she's speaking. My ears ring as if I am being held underwater. I start grabbing at the bracelet. "Get it off me," I whisper. Then louder, "Get it off me!"

Helene stills me and unclasps it.

I wrench it from her hand and hurl it into the fire, then fall to my knees. Sobs rack my body.

I curl my fists and hammer the floor with them. Someone is screaming. The sound makes my bones hurt.

"My lady . . ." Helene's soft voice breaks through the screams. "My lady, shhhhhh." She cups my face and shakes her head. "Shhhhh."

It was me. I was screaming.

I stumble to my feet and into the chair by the fire. Helene kneels in front of me. "Please, princess, tell me what has happened."

Barely able to breathe, still sobbing as I speak, I press my hands to my chest and stare down at her. "Thorne has betrayed me," I whisper. "He has betrayed me."

This time, I do not knock when I reach my father's study. It is early. I barely slept. Helene is holding me close, her arm around my waist. I push the door open and walk inside. Perhaps something is different about my stride today because he looks up as I enter.

He glances at Helene. He has never liked her, and his lips twitch with displeasure. Leaning on his elbows, he chews his lower lip and clicks his tongue impatiently.

I clear my throat. "Father . . ."

My father doesn't speak, just sits up and crosses his arms in front of his rotund stomach. Something moves behind me. A shadow. Helene's grip tightens on my arm, but I don't need to turn around to know who is there.

Thorne's scent, his presence, fills the room. He walks past me and stands beside my father. His lips stretch into a smile. I thought I knew the iterations of his face, but this one is different. It is laced with pity.

"It's all right, Calla, I've explained everything to your father."

My heart clenches tight in my chest. I look at Helene, but she is staring at Thorne with a stony expression. "You told him?" I ask, breathless with hope, hating myself for thinking that he might have confessed his love for me when I *know* – because I saw it with my own eyes – that he sees me as nothing but a pathetic plaything.

"I told him of your confession," Thorne says slowly. "But it's all right. Your father, in his wisdom, understands that these things happen. He will not punish you for your mistake."

I shake my head. I know I look wild and exhausted. My hair is unbrushed, knotted from tossing and turning on my pillows all night. There are dark circles beneath my eyes, and my skin is grey around the edges.

Every piece of me hurts. Right down to my soul.

I meet Thorne's gaze, and my entire body starts to shudder. "You told him we . . .?"

"I told him you confessed your love for me," Thorne says gently. "And that you were hoping I might stop the wedding."

Helene's grip is so hard now I can feel her fingernails digging into my flesh. My father's cheeks are flushed with rage, but he does not speak.

I hang my head and stare at my feet. Shame ricochets through my limbs.

I am broken.

IO

THORNE

For a moment, I thought it was all about to crumble. When I saw Calla's long blond locks disappearing through the door to the courtyard and realised she had seen me with Lucielle, I thought I'd allowed one moment of arrogant hedonism to ruin the *years* of preparation I've put into my scheme to become king.

But, once again, I seem to have come out unscathed.

When I told him Calla had developed a sad little crush and confessed her love for me, Magnus believed me without question.

When I told Lucielle I hadn't seen the bracelet and would buy her another, she simply batted her big, thick eyelashes at me and *thanked* me.

It wouldn't surprise me if Calla herself came crawling back to me later tonight and begged me to reconsider being her lover. If she does, I am confident I can win her around.

"This was the only way, my love," I'd tell her. "Lucielle was just part of the game. I intend to ask her to be Edmund's lover."

And Calla is so incredibly naive, and desperate to be loved, that she'd believe it. I can see her now, blinking up at me with those sea-green eyes, begging me to love her forever.

I might have been lying to Lucielle about making her my queen, but I was not lying when I said Calla would end up in the tower for the rest of her life.

Magnus will fall suddenly ill and sadly decline until he passes quietly in his sleep. Edmund will suffer a terrible accident.

And in the absence of any heirs, I will be in the wings, waiting to offer myself as his replacement.

For have I not proven my loyalty to both kingdoms? Have I not proven I am worthy?

I reach for the wine and pour myself another glass. Not long now. And I will take my rightful place as king.

II

CALLA

I am already a ghost. Floating through the castle as if I am not really here. I have been measured, fitted, talked to, prodded, and paraded. And I have done it all with a smile.

Thorne has not looked at me or spoken to me since that moment in my father's office, and I have not sought him out.

Though my instinct was to search for any small glimmer of hope I could find that might indicate I had made a mistake, every time I felt as if I was about to fall into that trap, I went to Helene instead.

Now, she sits beside me, holding my hand. "Are you ready, my lady?" she asks, sadness lacing her tone.

I nod, staring out at the bright full moon above the castle. "As ready as I'll ever be."

There is silence for a moment, then Helene says, "Thorne still intends to go with you to Xandor?"

"Yes. My father insists on it. He believes I am too fragile to be alone." I shake my head ruefully. "And Thorne is his *most* trusted adviser."

Helene sighs heavily. Then she stands and moves so she is positioned in front of me. She reaches into her pocket and withdraws a small velvet bag. Pressing it into my hand, she says, "Take this. Go to Lucielle. Offer her this in exchange for her alliance. Ask her to at least speak to your father and see that Thorne is not allowed to go with you."

I look down at the bag. "Whatever is inside here, she will not accept it. He has promised her a throne."

"He promised you a lot of things, too." Helene curls my fingers around the pouch. "You must try, my lady. I fear for your safety if Thorne follows you to Xandor. I fear for all of us if he is able to carry out his plan."

"Helene, what could you possibly . . .?" I open the pouch. Inside is the bracelet. The one I threw into the fire.

"Tell her what he told you. Tell her the promises he made you, the way he made you feel. Try to make her see that he is using her the same way he used you."

I trace the inscription with my index finger. "Helene . . ."

"My lady. You must *try*."

I inhale slowly, holding the air in my lungs. "I don't know where to find her."

"I have arranged for her to meet you in the very same courtyard where she rendezvoused with Thorne." Helene glances out of the window at the moon. "You should go now, princess, if you intend to go."

I stand slowly. For the past five days, I have felt lost. Without a purpose. Helpless. But now, a glimmer of hope has taken hold of me. I reach for my cloak and wrap it around my shoulders, then I nod briefly at Helene and hurry from the room.

In the courtyard, I wait by the fountain. Visions of Thorne and his lover right here, by the fountain, plague my thoughts. I try not to see them but every time I close my eyes, there they are. When she finally appears, she saunters towards me as if she has every intention of laughing in my face.

"Princess," she says, crossing her arms in front of her stomach. "This is an unexpected meeting."

I do not speak, simply take the pouch from my pocket and offer it to her. She smirks and opens it, tipping the bracelet into her hand. She blinks at it. The smirk wavers.

"How do you have this?" Her tone has sharpened.

"Thorne gave it to me when he promised to come to Xandor and spend his life with me."

"He was lying," she says quickly. "He was lying to you. He never intended to be yours. He promised me –"

"That he would love you? Protect you? Give you the world?" Defiance raises a cautious head, and when Lucielle's eyes narrow, it grows braver. "Did he tell you to wear this, so you'd know he was yours even if you weren't allowed to show it in public?"

Lucielle turns away from me and begins to pace back and forth.

"When exactly did he promise you'd be queen?"

She shakes her head, scraping her fingers through her hair. "Stop."

"Next year? Five years? Ten years? Twenty?"

Lucielle's hand curls around the bracelet. She shoves it into her pocket and spins back around to face me. "You're pathetic," she spits. "He used you. He never loved you."

"And do you truly believe he loved you?" I ask quietly.

Tutting, but refusing to answer the question, Lucielle pushes past me.

She's a few paces away when I shout, "He doesn't love you any more than he loves me, and you know it. Deep down, you know it!"

She stops, doesn't move. Then slowly she turns around.

She stares at me a moment, then launches for me. She shoves me, hard, but I saw her coming and I'm steadfast. I grab her shoulders and push her back, but she doesn't let go of me either.

I spin her around, claw at her face, and push again.

This time, she shrieks and falls backwards. Her skull collides with the basin of the fountain. It makes a loud cracking sound. Her eyes widen, and she drops to the floor. Blood immediately surrounds her, blooming from beneath the back of her head, trickling into the cobbled cracks of the courtyard.

She is still, and quiet.

I study her face. Now that she is not smirking, she is quite beautiful, really.

I wait for panic to grip me, but it doesn't come.

She is dead, and I killed her, and instead of feeling afraid or racked with inconsolable guilt, I feel . . . nothing.

Crouching down, I pry the bracelet from her fingers and check for a pulse. There is none. I push the dark curls from her face and tilt my head. She is completely different from me – dark hair, dark eyes, softer features.

But deep in my soul, as I look at her, I know that I was right. Thorne didn't love her and he didn't love me. He used us both. She was a pawn in his game, just as I was.

The only difference is, I didn't betray another woman in order to steal her crown.

A flicker of something close to pleasure lights in my belly as I think about Thorne's face when he discovers she is dead. But just as quickly as it rises, it's extinguished by tears.

What has he done to me? That I would rejoice in a serving girl, who got carried away with thoughts of jewels and status, losing her life? That I can sit here and feel no guilt, no shame, for causing it?

I reach out and adjust her cloak, pull it closer around her waist. As I move it, something catches the moonlight. A dagger. She brought a dagger to meet me. I pull it free from its sheath and press my index finger to the point. I am still crying when I hear footsteps behind me.

"She's dead," I spit, preparing to see Thorne when I turn around.

"Who is dead?"

"Edmund . . ." Fear thickens like ice in my veins. I stand, dagger in one hand, bracelet in the other.

"I followed her. I saw her sneaking out here and I thought . . ." He steps closer, then kneels beside Lucielle. "What did you do?" he mutters. He is staring at her and the blood. He looks up at me and sees the knife. Lucielle's blood slicks his palm.

"Edmund, I didn't do this. Listen to me. Thorne –"

"You killed her? You discovered I was fucking her, and you killed her?"

My mouth hangs open. I shake my head, staring down at him. "I've known you were fucking her since the night of the banquet, Edmund but I did *not* kill her. It was an accident. She and Thorne were –"

"You're crazy!" Edmund yells.

"Please." I grab his sleeve. "Listen to me."

He shakes me off. "You'll pay for this." His hand goes to his waist, searching for his own blade. "I'll have your head." He takes out his weapon.

My fingers tighten on the handle of Lucielle's knife. Edmund looks up at me. But before he can spring to his feet, I lurch forward and plunge the blade into his neck.

Edmund gasps and raises his hands to the wound. He drops his own weapon, grapples for the blade, and pulls it free.

With it comes a torrent of blood. It sprays onto my clothes, into my hair, and onto my face.

He slouches back, trembling. His eyes are wide, his mouth open, his face draining of colour.

Slowly, as Edmund watches me with his last few lifeless breaths, I place one blade into his hand and one into Lucielle's. Then I drop the bracelet between them.

Edmund tries to speak.

I tweak my index finger beneath his chin. "When they find you, they'll read this scene, and do you know what they will conclude?"

Edmund exhales a rattling breath. He coughs, and blood trickles down his chin.

"They will conclude that Thorne and Lucielle were lovers, and that you became jealous. That you attacked her, and that you killed one another." I shrug, straightening myself up, looking down at my dress which has turned from white to pale red.

"Or perhaps they will think Thorne killed you both." I shrug.

Edmund's eyes flutter and he slumps sideways.

"Either way, you're not going to be king, Edmund."

12

CALLA

I am sitting in front of the fire staring at my hands when Helene finds me. "Princess?" she asks quietly. "Did the meeting go well?"

I flex my fingers. "There's no blood." I turn them over and show them to her. "But it feels as if there is blood."

Helene swallows hard and kneels before me. "Calla," she whispers, using my name instead of my title for the first time in all the years we have known one another. "Please, tell me what happened."

"Edmund and Lucielle are dead. She fell, banged her head. He found us. I stabbed him."

"You . . ." Helene's words trail off. She rubs her palms over her face and shakes her head.

"I put the knife in her hand. When they're found, it will look as if –"

"You're not safe." Helene stands and drags me to my feet. "Calla, you must leave. You are not safe here."

I feel as if I am in a dream – or a nightmare. Everything is moving in slow motion. In the courtyard, as I watched them both die, power surged through me. I felt the most alive I have ever felt.

Now, I feel numb.

"Helene, it's all right." I try to smile. "They won't know it was me."

"Thorne will know. He'll know."

"He won't."

"He *will*, but even if he doesn't, you'll never be safe now. With Edmund dead before the wedding, his plans are in tatters. Who knows what he will do?"

I blink slowly at her. The numbness is fading. Panic grips my limbs. "What do I do? Where do I go?"

Helene rushes to my wardrobe and grabs a bag. Shoving clothes into it, she hisses, "I know someone who can help you. Keep you safe. Some call her a witch, a sorceress. To me, she is . . ." Helene turns and smiles at me. "She is my sister. She will protect you."

"Where? Where do I go?"

Helene plucks her own cloak from the hook behind the door. "I'll take you now. Is there anything you want to bring with you? Any memento or trinket?"

I turn slowly, assessing the room in which I have spent almost my entire life. Not a single reminder of joy jumps out at me. Thorne gave me joy. He was the first to bring a true smile to my lips, and the first to make me feel like more than just a princess.

My heart aches for him, and it burns *because* of him.

"No. There is nothing here I need."

Helene nods with solemn understanding, her eyes mirroring the storm of emotions brewing inside me. Without another word, she seizes my hand and leads me through the familiar, dimly lit corridors of the castle. The walls feel like they're closing in. I can hardly breathe, and if she wasn't with me, I'm not sure I'd ever find the bravery to leave.

We reach the servant's entrance, a forgotten door hidden behind thick tapestries. Its hinges groan in protest as we push through. The air outside bites at our skin, the wind howling. The sky, a canvas of dark, ominous clouds, looms overhead, threatening a storm.

I stop in the doorway and grip the side of the wall. "I'm not sure I can do this."

Helene turns to me, hair blowing in the wind. "Yes, you can." She takes my hands and squeezes them tightly. "You're stronger than you know, Calla. You always have been."

I stare at her and nod, even though I don't feel what she's feeling.

I don't feel brave; I never have.

But then I remember the way I felt when I was standing over Edmund and Lucielle, watching the life drain from their bodies, and something shifts deep in my core.

Once again, I search for guilt or sorrow and find none. They were terrible people. They wronged me, and now they are dead.

Helene tugs my wrist. "Calla, come."

My heart races as we run across the yard and through the large archway that leads to the clifftop path. Each beat is a thunderous echo that drowns out the sound of our hurried footsteps.

It takes a long time to make it to the cliffs. From the castle, in the moonlight, a guard could easily spot us – two cloaked figures fleeing across the marsh. Several times, I trip and Helene catches me. The hem of my dress is sodden and caked with mud. My arms too, and my boots.

When the cliffs come into view, curving round so their

jagged outlines cut into the brooding sky, I turn to her and stop. "Where are we going?"

Helene grips my hand and leads me towards the edge.

Above, thunder rumbles the promise of an oncoming deluge. I look down. The sea below rages, its waves crashing against the rocks with relentless fury, as if trying to climb the cliffs and reach for me. Down in the docks, Edmund's ship sits silent and dark.

"You have to climb down." Helene puts her hands on my shoulders and turns me so I am facing her. "If you climb down from this spot here, there is a cave. Swing yourself into it. My sister waits."

"Climb?" My eyes widen. "I can't –"

"I witnessed you climbing trees as a child, Calla. Yes, you can."

I look down at my dress. It is too heavy. Too cumbersome. Pulling off the cloak, I thrust it into Helene's arms, then turn around and ask her to unlace me.

She does as I ask.

When I tug the garment free and let it drop to the floor, standing in just my long underwear and corset, I shiver.

Helene smiles. "See," she says, "you are already finding yourself."

I brace my hands on my hips and breathe in deeply. The wind licks my cheeks, and moisture from the sea spray below soothes my skin.

"You must be brave, Calla," Helene's voice barely rises above the wind. "The path you take tonight is treacherous, and the future uncertain. But remember, you are strong. You will survive this."

I nod, my eyes stinging not from the biting wind but from the realisation that I might not see Helene again. She strokes my cheek, then inhales sharply and points to the cliff. "I'll help you. There are plenty of footholds on the way down. I've done it myself."

"If they find out you helped me escape..."

Helene puts a finger to her lips. "Shhhhh, child. I can take care of myself."

I back up to the cliffs and kneel down. Helene stands over me and instructs me to lower myself over and keep my grip on the clifftop until I have a firm foothold.

Dangling here, jutting out above the ocean, I wonder what would happen if I let go. I could fall into the ocean's embrace and end it all. Right now.

But the fire in my belly will not let me. I have come too far to give up now, and I have seen a glimpse of the power I could have if I shake my royal chains.

"Goodbye." I look up, but Helene has gone.

I am truly alone.

13

CALLA

By the time I reach the place where the cliff falls away and becomes a cave instead, my arms are burning and my legs are shaking. It is raining. Water stings my cheeks, and the ocean roars beneath me.

I do not know if I have the strength to swing myself inside as Helene told me to, so I stay there, clinging on by my fingertips, heart beating so fast it feels like it might be ripped from my chest at any moment.

Finally, I find the gumption to do what needs to be done.

With a scream that rises above the wind, I swing back, then hurl myself into the gaping hole in the cliff.

I land in a heap on the floor. Rough stone scrapes my forearms and my palms. My body throbs and aches. Slowly, my eyes begin to adjust to the light. It is green, shimmering as if it is reflecting water onto the ceiling of the cave. Except, there is no water here, just stone.

I stand up, using the slick cave wall to steady myself, and walk deeper into the eerie light.

"Princess, I have been waiting for you." A female voice – older than Helene's but of a similar tone – drifts towards me. I strain my eyes, staring into the shadows, but can see no one.

I keep walking, and then a fire comes into view. Flickering flames, green and hypnotic, dance up towards the ceiling.

I crouch in front of them and extend my hands to warm them.

I am staring into the fire when a figure appears through the flames. On the other side of the fire, an old woman in a long green dress stares at me. She has silver hair that reaches her waist, and hands that look younger than her face.

Her eyes are a bright, sparkling blue.

"You are Helene's sister?"

"My name is Elowen." The woman walks slowly around the fire until she reaches me, then extends both hands and helps me to my feet. "You have had a hard journey."

"It was not so bad," I tell her. "Across the moors, then down the cliff face. The climbing was the most difficult."

Elowen smiles softly. She tilts her head and says, "I was not referring to your journey from the castle. I was referring to your journey into womanhood."

I flinch a little at the expression. Thorne's face flashes in front of my eyes. Then Lucielle's. The fountain. Edmund. The dagger. Blood. Fucking. Laughing. The bracelet. The words he promised were mine but were meant for another.

I screw my eyes closed, and tears congeal in my throat.

When I open them again, I'm crying. Elowen nods slowly. "You were wronged, my child," she says. "I can help you right that wrong. But you must choose your path."

She turns and walks to a line of small glass vials set on a shelf which has been carved into the rock. She picks two of them, then returns to me. "In my left hand, I hold vengeance. In my right, I hold peace."

My eyes catch on the bottle in her right hand. "Peace?" My mind returns to the ocean, to the way I felt when I contemplated giving myself to her murky depths. But when I look at the other bottle, something else happens. My skin warms, flickers, tingles. Rage and heartbreak dance in the cracks between my bones. But instead of pain I feel . . . desire.

The desire to make those who have wronged me understand exactly what they took.

Elowen returns the peace bottle to the shelf. "You have decided," she says. "You decided before you even left the castle that you would no longer be a victim." She presses the vial into my hand.

The liquid inside is ink-black and moves slowly as I stare at it. "If I drink this . . .?"

"You will be given the power you seek."

"What does that mean?"

"What would you like it to mean?"

I press my lips together and begin to pace the floor. Thorne's words bore into my skull. *You can never be mine, but I can be yours. Go to Edmund. Take me with you. I love you.*

Anger sweeps through me. It is so powerful it feels it might crack me open. "I want to rip out his heart the way he ripped out mine! I want them to pay. All of them. Every single person who ever doubted me or belittled me or used me as if I'm nothing but an object for their own pleasure or greed."

A slow smile parts Elowen's lips. She nods. "Drink the potion and it shall be so."

Without hesitation, I rip off the cap and tip my head back. I drink it down in one gulp, and it burns like acid as it tears down my throat towards my stomach. Like fire and ice, it swirls inside me.

My chest tightens. My breath hitches. My body constricts. All of it. The fire and the ice trickle down my limbs, and up my spine, and through my veins. My head tips violently backwards and my jaw opens. A scream breaks free from deep inside my soul. It fills the cave, bouncing off the walls so I swallow it back down.

Pain takes me over. It grows and grows until it is so strong I fear I can't take anymore. And then it is over. As it subsides, a strange sense of calm blankets me. My limbs, though quivering slightly, feel laced with a newfound strength. The cave, once dimly lit, now glistens with a clarity that wasn't there before. The shimmering green light dances across my skin, casting ethereal reflections that seem to pulse and vibrate.

Elowen watches me closely, her eyes reflecting a mixture of pride and something else – a kind of ancient knowing. "You are becoming, my child," she whispers.

"Becoming . . . what?" I ask.

"What they made you," she replies, striding towards me and cupping my face in her hands. "You are becoming the destroyer of men. The one who will right the wrongs done to women like you. You are becoming an angel of death."

Angel of death.

I tilt my head back and, this time, I laugh.

The potion continues its work. It feels as if it's weaving through my very being, untangling the knots of my old self and knitting together a new, stronger version. My senses heighten; I can hear the distant roar of the ocean as if she is whispering secrets just for me. The scent of the earthy cave, the tang of the sea, the crackle of the fire.

When I look down, my dress seems to be growing larger, longer, fuller. The bloodstains left by Edmund and Lucielle pale and spread, turning it a muted shade of pink.

Like the rose Edmund tossed aside.

As I run my hands over the fabric, suddenly, my vision

sharpens. I feel as if I'm seeing not just with my eyes, but with my entire being. As if I can move through the world in a completely different way now; as if I can control it.

Elowen approaches the fire. From her pocket, she takes a handful of something that looks like silver dust. She holds it in her palm, then opens her fingers and blows the dust into the flames. A moment later, she rolls up her sleeve and thrusts her hand into the fire.

I watch with curiosity. Her expression does not change. She is not in pain.

Slowly, she draws back her arm and, when she turns around, she holds a bow and a quiver of arrows in her hands. The bow is unlike any I've seen before – it shimmers with the same ethereal light that now seems to radiate from me. "This is for you," she says, handing me the bow and arrows. "With these, your aim will be true, and your purpose clear. You are no longer just Calla. You are the justice-bringer. Your arrows will carry your will, and men's hearts will quiver at your whisper."

I take the bow, and it feels like an extension of my own body, light yet unbreakable. I test its string, and the sound it makes resonates with the core of my soul.

"From this moment, any man who has harmed a woman will be yours to destroy."

Joy bubbles in my stomach. "I will avenge them."

"But only . . ." Elowen smiles. "Only when that man is truly happy will you be able to take his life. He must be in love, experiencing a moment of utter contentment." She gestures to the bow and arrow. "That is when you will appear before him to exact your revenge."

"Thorne," I mutter. Frustration momentarily swallows the joy I was feeling. "I must wait until he is in love?"

Elowen nods slowly. "It will be worth the wait, my child.

Trust me. It will be worth the wait." Her gaze meets mine, and in her eyes, I see a reflection of the new me – a creature of both beauty and terror. A creature capable of being all the things they told me I would never be.

I am the ethereal avenger, and my journey has just begun.

14

THORNE

I wake from a sound, peaceful sleep and cross the room to find the chamber pot. Rubbing my eyes, my gaze lands on the doorway. In the dim candlelight, I see a slip of paper protruding from beneath the door itself.

Pulling up my trousers, I pick it up and hold it to the light.

Dearest Thorne,

Calla has asked to meet with me. I have taken my blade. I will not let her turn me against you.

Lucielle x

My heart jumps violently behind my ribs. Stupid girl. Stupid, stupid girl. She'll ruin us both! Everything I have done, grooming her, coaxing her, from organising a deliberate failed assassination, to seducing her. She will see that all my work is undone, I can't allow that.

Without even stopping for a shirt or cloak, I throw open

the door and pound down the corridor towards the courtyard. As I approach, my footsteps slow. Something deep in my gut tells me things are not as they should be.

I look down when my foot slips on something. A smear of blood on the stone floor.

Bracing myself, I push open the door to the courtyard. If Lucielle has killed the princess, my entire plan will have gone to waste. Perhaps I shouldn't have trusted a brainless serving girl with –

I stop in the shadow of the doorway.

Moonlight streams down into the courtyard illuminating a scene that, for all the world, looks as though it should only exist on stage at a theatre.

Lucielle lies on the floor, blood pooling behind her dark curls. Beside her, Edmund has slumped sideways. His throat has been slashed, and his body is so drenched in blood that barely an inch of skin is visible.

Each of them holds a knife.

I stride forward, careful not to tread close enough to bloody my shoes.

The bracelet . . . It lies between them.

My mind races. Lucielle was meeting Calla. Did she do this? My lips twitch. I am almost impressed. Finally, Magnus's perfect princess found a backbone.

Tiptoeing forward, I reach for the bracelet and drop it into my pocket. As I run my fingers over the cool, gold band, rage tears through me. I fight the urge to scream at the sky.

Edmund dead. Lucielle dead, and Calla? Where is Calla?

I leave the courtyard and race to the princess's chambers. They are empty. The fire is dying in the grate.

"She is gone." The dulcet tone of Calla's chambermaid floats over from the shadows. When she steps into the light, she has folded her arms in front of her stomach and is staring at me. "You will never see her again, Thorne."

"You have hidden her from me?"

"You do not deserve to set eyes on her again. For as long as you live –"

I do not let her finish. Simply turn around and slam the door behind me.

As I head for Magnus's chambers, my lips twitch into a smile. I know what I must do to save myself.

I will still be king.

15

THORNE
ONE YEAR LATER

The silk of my dress robes feels smooth under my fingertips, luscious . . . *regal*. The jewels on my cloak are heavy, and they gleam as they catch the light of the fire. Staring at my reflection in the mirror, I raise a glass and toast myself.

"After all you went through," I say, shaking my head in disbelief, "you pulled it off. You actually pulled it off."

Today, I was named Edmund's successor, betrothed to his cousin Rose in a union of loyalty and power because of the support and strength I showed in the aftermath of Edmund's death.

"Didn't need Calla after all," I mutter, drinking down half the glass, then refilling it. I set the glass down on the mantel, then adjust the intricate silver embroidery on my robe, a reflection of my newfound status. The room is silent, save for the quiet rustling of fabric and my own steady breaths. It's a silence that speaks volumes, the calm before the storm of festivities to commence this evening.

A knock on the door breaks the stillness. "My lord, the feast

78

begins shortly, and Lady Rose should like to converse with you before its commencement," a servant announces from the other side.

Lady Rose . . . a fine specimen of a woman. Dark hair, like Lucielle's. Plump lips. Far more shapely than Calla, and far more spirited. It turns out, to my surprise, I quite like a spirited woman.

"Thank you, I will be out shortly. Please tell Lady Rose I will be with her momentarily," I respond before drinking down the last of the wine.

Smoothing my hair and beard, I assess myself one final time, then turn on my heel to approach the door.

Before I can reach it, the room feels suddenly colder, the air charged with a tension I can't quite place. I scan the room, my senses heightened.

I turn slowly back to the mirror, and then I see her.

Calla.

She stands in the shadowed corner of the room, her green eyes piercing through the dim light. I spin back around but before I can stride over to her, she steps out of her hiding place.

"How did you get here?" I demand, reaching for my dagger.

She says nothing, simply walks towards me as if she is gliding on ice. Her dress is pale and pink. It floats behind her almost like the train on a wedding dress.

"Thorne," she replies, her voice steady and sharp. "You look splendid in your dress robes, ready to embrace a crown that was never meant for you. Congratulations."

"Leave. Now. Or I will see you are thrown in the tower for the rest of your pathetic life."

Calla stops. She tilts her head and smiles but the rest of her face is strangely still. "No, Thorne. You've said enough, done enough. I don't wish to hear your threats."

My words falter in my throat. I try to speak, but I cannot.

"Today, you stand at the precipice of power, but remember this – power built on betrayal can never last. I am here to remind you that actions have consequences. One day, you will learn the weight of yours."

Her confidence, her intensity, is unlike the Calla I knew. There's a fierceness in her gaze, a resolve that sends a shiver down my spine. "You cannot frighten me, Calla."

She smiles, a smile that doesn't reach her eyes. "You may not fear me now, but you will. When the time comes, you will remember this moment, and all the ones that came before when you could have made different choices. Been a better man."

Before I can respond, before I can reach out or call for the guards, she steps back into the shadow, disappearing as if she were never there, leaving no trace but the echo of her words and a cold dread that settles in my heart.

16

CALLA

FIFTEEN YEARS LATER

They look so peaceful. Her hair is dark, like Lucielle's was. Glimmers of silvery grey have started to appear in the locks closest to her face. They frame her cheeks like a halo.

He is still dark and handsome, almost as if he hasn't aged. His beard is neatly trimmed. His chest is bare, and it occurs to me I only ever saw him that way once.

Rose turns over and rests her head on his shoulder. He kisses her forehead, not even waking, then laces his fingers with hers. He squeezes them as if even in his sleep he cannot hold her close enough or long enough.

I catch a glimpse of myself in the mirror above the fireplace. I have not aged a day. My skin is perfect, even smoother than it was in my other life, and my hair hangs long and loose over my shoulders. I breathe out slowly and an icy breeze drifts through the room, toying with the thin curtains that hang around the grand four-poster bed.

A bed fit for a king.

Rose turns away from Thorne and pulls the blankets closer

around her. "Darling," she murmurs, "would you stoke the fire? It's cold."

"Of course, my love." He kisses her shoulder. He's about to turn over and get out of bed, then he pauses. He sits up.

"Is everything all right, my darling?"

He stares at her. His eyes soften. He shakes his head. "I love you," he whispers.

Frowning, Rose laughs. She has a lovely laugh. Like water babbling over rocks in a brook. "I know," she says.

"No . . ." He clasps her hand, tight, as if he's afraid she's going to disappear. "I *truly* love you." He kisses her. It is a deep kiss. She leans into him, and he reaches for her nightdress, tugging it over her head.

I smile, flexing my fingers on the shiny silver bow I hold in my hand. Then I load an arrow and fire it into the side of Rose's neck.

It pierces the vein exactly where I intended it to. Her eyes spring wide, but only for a second. She doesn't even scream. Just slumps forward as a crimson river of blood gushes down her chest.

Thorne opens his eyes, whispers her name, moves to pull out the arrow, then stops because he knows it will make the blood flow faster.

He pulls her into his lap and stares down at her, smoothing her hair from her face, tears streaming.

I breathe in deeply. I have waited so long to feel his heart breaking, and I want to savour the moment for as long as I can before –

He opens his mouth to call for help, and I step out of the shadows. "She's gone," I say quietly.

Thorne looks from Rose to me. He rubs his eyes, smearing blood across his face. "It can't be . . ." he whispers, clenching the blankets with pale knuckles. He opens his mouth to speak, but before the sound can leave his mouth, I click my fingers and remove his voice. He clasps his throat with both hands, tries to scream again, stares down at Rose then back at me with wild, terrified eyes that make my vicious heart sing with pride.

Positioning himself in front of her, shifting her lifeless body onto the mattress, he points at me. "Witch," he mouths.

I glide closer. "Witch?" A broad smile parts my lips. A true smile. The kind of smile *he* used to coax from me. "Oh no, Thorne. I am no witch." My hand goes to the smooth leather that sits snug against my chest. I trace it all the way up to my shoulder, then reach for an arrow. Plucking it from its quiver, I prepare the bow.

Thorne kneels, holding the sheets to cover his modesty.

"I am something far more deadly than a witch." I raise the bow and stare at the place on his chest beneath which his rotten heart beats. "I am the woman you scorned." I pull back my arm, feeling the tension deep in my bones.

Thorne lifts his hands. The smell of urine fills the air.

"You are pathetic," I spit. Then I look at Rose. "But you loved her, didn't you?"

Thorne nods.

I let go.

The arrow flies forward and spears his chest in exactly the right place. He gasps and his eyes widen. It buries itself up to the fletching. I lower the bow, then raise my free hand and stalk closer. I step around the bed.

Thorne cannot move, but his eyes follow me as I climb onto the bed and kneel in front of him. "Do you have any last words?"

Blood trickles from the corner of his mouth.

A laugh swells in my chest. I curl my lithe fingers around

the arrow, close my eyes, and pull. When I open them again, a still-throbbing hearts quivers on the end of my weapon.

I hold it close to my chest. It beats against me, and the blood seeps gloriously into my gown. As Thorne falls backwards onto the bed, I turn to Rose and thrust my hand into her chest. My fingers part her skin like blades, cracking her ribs so I can tear out her warm, naive heart.

"You shouldn't have trusted him," I tell her.

Holding a heart in each hand, I keep them cradled against my chest until they have forgotten how to be alive.

As the colour bleeds from them into my dress, they become ever paler, and harder. Until, like fragile bones, they shatter when I drop them to the floor.

I could be free now, if I chose it. But Thorne was just the beginning. My rage is far from vanquished, and I will never stop.

EPILOGUE

"Zakron, a once prosperous kingdom, has been a crumbling ruin for over five hundred years. Its ruin came about from a King that cared more for riches and wealth than his own people, even his own daughter.

For when her heart was broken she cursed that kingdom, so that they would suffer the agonising heartbreak she was forced to endure.

When one truly gave their heart to another, she would appear, in vengeful, spectral form with a bow and arrow. From those shadows she would pierce the heart of anyone who dared give their love to another."

Jordell Torvin, Legends of Levanthria, 260KR

AFTERWORD

I hope you enjoyed this dark retelling inspired by Cupid. It has been a blast to work with an author as talented as Cara Clare on this story. I just want to take an opportunity to thank you Cara for helping bring this story to life. This was the first time I have worked with another author in my story world and it has been fantastic to see you embrace the brutal world of Levanthria.

Another thing I am often asked for is for A Forest Of Bastards And Betrayal to be available in print. For that reason You can read it as a bonus story on the next page.

Enjoy

A FOREST OF BASTARDS AND BETRAYAL

By A.P Beswick

SPOILER WARNING

A Forest Of Bastards And Betrayal should not be read until you have finished A Forest Of Vanity And Valour.
You have been warned, seriously do not turn the page if you have not finished the first book in the Levanthria series as this will contain spoilers.

A FOREST OF BASTARDS AND BETRAYAL

The Hidden Chapter

The rough rope bites into my wrists, chafing my skin as I stumble out of the cart, half-dragged by the merciless guards. My vision is blurred, but the sound of Codrin's voice is unmistakable. He's a large, muscular elf with pitch-black skin, a cruel sneer, and an unforgiving temperament. His eyes seem to pierce through me, as if he relishes in my suffering. I've been captured and dragged before this assembly against my will, and the humiliation is unbearable.

"Coward," I spit at Codrin, the saliva striking his face. I can see the anger in his eyes, dark and menacing like a brewing storm. The muscles in his jaw clench, and his fists tighten as if he is barely restraining himself. But I have no fear. I've faced worse, and I've had Vireo by my side. Through all the challenges we've faced, the bond between us has grown stronger, and I cling to that connection now, even as I stand before my tormentor.

Then Morgana moves in front of me, her presence commanding the attention of everyone present. She walks with a confident, predatory stride, each step calculated and graceful, as though she owns the very ground beneath her feet. Her long, wavy red hair frames her pale face like a fiery halo, a stark contrast to her cold, calculating eyes that seem to bore into my very soul.

Her dark robes billow around her like a cloud of evil, their shadows seeming to swallow the light around her. She wears a plunging black dress that clings to her form, revealing and concealing in equal measure, only adding to her sinister allure. Morgana's cruelty knows no bounds, and as she draws near, I instinctively brace myself for whatever torment she has in store for me.

I know of her power, the sorceress who manipulates the minds of men, twisting them to her whim and breaking their wills as easily as snapping a twig. I steel myself, determined not to let her break me, but the fear gnaws at the edges of my resolve.

As she raises her hand and begins to weave her spell, a searing pain rips through my mind, like a thousand needles piercing my skull. It's agony, and I grit my teeth, trying to resist. I think of Vireo, of our friendship and our shared cause, but the pain only grows worse. Morgana's power is relentless, her magic fuelled by her unyielding desire for control and domination, and I find myself struggling against the tide of her malevolent influence.

Morgana's jagged voice echoes in my head, invasive and unyielding, a cruel and relentless litany of blame. Her voice slithers through my thoughts like a venomous snake, aggressive and malicious. She twists my memories, turns them against me, forcing me to see Vireo as the cause of all my pain and suffering. I try to fight it, but the pain is overwhelming.

In my mind, I revisit the days filled with laughter and camaraderie shared with Vireo and Gillam. Memories of our victories and the bonds forged in the heat of battle surface, but Morgana's magic corrupts them, replacing the joy and triumph with pain and suffering. Our brotherhood is poisoned by the insidious influence of her spell, and I feel the darkness gnawing at the edges of my soul.

"He abandoned you," she whispers, her voice a serpent's hiss in my ear, dripping with venom. "He left you to this fate, knowing full well what would happen. He never cared for you, only for his own selfish desires."

I want to scream, to deny her words, but the pain is unbearable. My thoughts are a whirlwind of confusion, and I can no longer tell where Morgana's lies end and the truth begins.

Her words coil around my heart like a constrictor, tightening their grip and suffocating the love and loyalty I once held for my friends. I am left with nothing but the bitterness and despair that Morgana has planted within me.

"No," I strain to say, my voice hoarse and weak, fighting back against the relentless torrent of Morgana's intrusive thoughts. "You're wrong. Vireo... he would never abandon me."

But Morgana's grip on my mind is relentless, and her malicious whispers continue to assault my spirit. I push back as best as I can, desperately clinging to the memories of our shared laughter, the victories we've achieved together, and the unwavering bond that has defined our friendship.

"Vireo... Gillam... our brotherhood is stronger than your lies!" I shout, even as my voice threatens to break under the weight of the pain. "I won't let you take that from me!"

For a moment, I feel a flicker of resistance, a spark of defiance that refuses to be extinguished. But Morgana is relentless, and her magic bears down on me with crushing force. Despite my efforts to fight back, the pain intensifies, and the darkness continues to seep into every corner of my mind.

As I struggle to hold onto the love and loyalty that once defined me, I can feel Morgana's malevolent influence slowly eroding my resolve. The strength I once had to resist her is fading, and it feels as though I'm drowning in a sea of despair and betrayal.

Morgana continues to burrow into the darkened depths of my mind, her magic seeping through every crack and crevice like a poisonous mist. The excruciating pain tears through me, causing every muscle in my body to tense and tremble. My jaw clenches, and I grind my teeth together as I try to force her malignant presence back.

Her voice weaves a cruel tapestry of deceit within my thoughts, aggressive tones and words with a ruthless and spiked tongue. "He abandoned you," she hisses, the words echoing through my skull like a venomous chant. "Vireo left you."

The pain intensifies, driving me to the edge of madness. It feels as though hot needles are being driven into my brain, each one searing a new pathway for Morgana's lies to follow. "You lost everything because of him," she continues, her voice insidious and relentless. "He sacrificed you."

My thoughts grow darker, consumed by the shadows cast by Morgana's spell. The line between reality and manipulation blurs, her twisted words entwining with my own memories and fears. The pain is unbearable, but even worse is the creeping sense of doubt that begins to take root within me. Could it be true? Did Vireo abandon me, betray me for his own selfish gains?

I try to hold on to the love and trust that once bound us together, the memories of shared laughter and hard-won victories that defined our friendship. But Morgana's magic is relentless, eroding my resolve like a river carving its way through stone. The pain, the doubt, the betrayal – it all blends together, an inescapable cacophony of torment that threatens to drown me.

As I struggle to fight back, I feel my strength waning, the last flickers of hope snuffed out by the inexorable advance of Morgana's power. My thoughts turn darker still, consumed by the bitterness and despair that she has planted within me.

"He abandoned you," she whispers again, her voice now indistinguishable from my own thoughts. "Vireo left you."

And in the darkest recesses of my mind, where the line between truth and manipulation has all but vanished, I find myself starting to believe her.

With every ounce of strength I have left, I make one last vain attempt to repel Morgana's magic and hold onto the now fading and corrupted memories of my once friend and ally. My voice, barely a whisper, trembles with desperation and pain as I call out to the depths of my soul.

"Vireo... help me. Please..."

Images of our shared battles, laughter, and camaraderie flash through my mind, flickering like dying embers in a storm. I focus on those memories, trying to keep them from being consumed by the darkness that Morgana has unleashed within me.

But it feels as though I am grasping at smoke, the memories slipping through my fingers like sand. The pain is overwhelming, and my resolve weakens with each passing moment.

As the last vestiges of hope and loyalty fade, I am left with the bitter taste of Morgana's lies, wondering if anything I once believed in was ever real.

I want to scream, to deny her words, but the pain is unbearable. My thoughts are a whirlwind of confusion, and I can no longer tell where Morgana's lies end and the truth begins. Her insidious whispers slither through my mind, entangling themselves around every memory, every moment of friendship I had shared with Vireo.

As the pain intensifies, it feels as if my very soul is being ripped apart. My heartbeat quickens, each pulse driving the agony deeper into my being. Sweat beads on my forehead, my breathing ragged and uneven.

In the end, I can take no more. With a final, desperate sob, I succumb to her manipulation. My once ironclad loyalty to Vireo shatters, replaced by a deep-seated hatred and resentment. The jagged shards of our broken bond cut deep, fuelling the fire of betrayal within me.

Vireo has betrayed me, left me to suffer at the hands of these cruel people. The thought consumes me, fuelled by the magic that now twists my thoughts and feelings. Morgana has won, and I am nothing more than a pawn in her cruel game.

As I stand here, shackled and broken, my heart heavy with the weight of my newfound hatred, I vow to make Vireo pay for his betrayal. The cold steel of vengeance replaces the warmth of friendship, and a dark determination takes hold of me, driving me forward.

No matter the cost, no matter the sacrifice, I will see Vireo suffer as I have suffered. I will exact my revenge, even if it means my own destruction. For I have nothing left to lose, and everything to gain from Morgana's magic has awoken my true feelings my true thoughts on that coward that I once called friend. In the end, all that remains of the man I once was is a burning desire for retribution, and I will not rest until it is achieved.

Morgana's cold, calculating gaze settles upon me, her piercing eyes seeming to see straight through my soul. I stand before her, my posture submissive, my newfound loyalty to her unbreakable. She has complete control over me now, and I am powerless to resist.

"You have done well, Lek," she says, her voice smooth as silk, yet laced with a sinister undertone. "You have embraced the truth and seen through Vireo's treachery. Now, you will help me bring him to justice."

I nod my head, my eyes burning with the hatred that now consumes me. Vireo has betrayed me, abandoned me in my hour of need. He has left me to suffer at the hands of these cruel people, and I will make him pay.

"Vireo will be coming soon," Morgana continues, her eyes narrowing as she gazes into the distance. "He will be unaware of your newfound knowledge of his betrayal, and we must use this to our advantage. You will lie in wait for him, Lek, and when the opportunity presents itself, you will strike him down."

My heart clenches at the thought, but I push aside any lingering doubts or feelings of loyalty. This is what Vireo deserves, for all the pain he has caused me. I will not hesitate to carry out Morgana's orders.

"I understand," I reply, my voice steady and determined. "Vireo will not suspect a thing, and when the time comes, I will bring him to his knees."

Morgana's lips curl into a cruel smile, and I can see the satisfaction in her eyes. She knows she has me in her grasp, and she relishes in the power she holds over me.

"Good," she says, her voice dripping with malicious intent. "Remember, Lek, Vireo is cunning and resourceful. You must be patient and bide your time. Do not let your hatred cloud your judgment, or else you may miss your chance to strike."

Her words echo through my mind, a constant reminder of the task that lies ahead. My hatred for Vireo, my once friend and ally, now fuels my every action. I cannot let this opportunity slip through my fingers.

"I will not fail you, Morgana," I assure her, my voice filled with conviction. "Vireo will pay for his betrayal, and I will see to it personally."

Morgana nods, her expression unreadable as she regards me with an appraising eye. "I have no doubt that you will succeed, Lek. Your hatred for Vireo is a powerful weapon, and one that I am confident you will wield with deadly precision."

I bow my head, acknowledging her words. The weight of my task settles heavily upon my shoulders, and I feel a grim determination settle within me. Vireo will pay for his betrayal, and I will be the instrument of his downfall.

As I prepare myself for the confrontation that lies ahead, my thoughts are filled with the memories of our once strong friendship, now twisted and corrupted by the darkness that Morgana has sown. In the end, all that remains is the hatred that now drives me, and the unyielding desire for revenge.

And so, I wait, my heart filled with a cold, bitter resolve. When Vireo comes, I will be ready, and I will not rest until he has paid the ultimate price for his betrayal.

As I lie in wait, feigning unconsciousness on the cold, hard ground, my great axe buried in the dirt just inches from my outstretched hand, time seems to slow to a crawl. The still air around me is heavy with anticipation, as the setting sun casts a warm glow over the scene, bathing everything in a golden light. My heartbeat is steady and calm, echoing in my ears like the rhythmic beating of a battle drum. Every beat serves as a reminder of the vengeance that awaits Vireo. The pulsating pressure that builds within my head serves as a constant reminder of Morgana's influence, her magic still coursing through my veins. I feel an eerie sense of calm settle over me, despite the gravity of the task at hand. And so, I bide my time, my body tense and ready to spring into action the moment Vireo reveals himself.

As I lie in wait, feigning unconsciousness on the cold, hard ground, I strain to hear the conversation between Vireo and Jareb. Through squinted eyes, I try to make out their shapes, but I can only discern faint outlines. The shadow of Vireo's hooded figure greets me first, and I can sense that he has not come alone. Jareb's voice carries through the air, mocking Vireo.

"Is it bravery or stupidity that brings you here tonight?" Jareb taunts.

Vireo's gaze shifts from me to the limp body of Laith, and I can feel Jareb's surprise at the concern Vireo seems to show for us. He continues to ridicule Vireo, while the wind whips Vireo's cloak behind him. Even in this dire situation, Vireo appears calm, confident or is it arrogance.

"You're pathetic!" Jareb growls. "Are you ready to face your judgment, Vireo?"

"Will you keep your word and let these men go?" Vireo demands.

Jareb's response is cold and calculating. "That is what I have proposed, is it not? Your life in exchange for theirs. A fair exchange indeed. Although I must admit the scrawny one on the left may not be of use to anyone for a while."

I can feel the tension in the air as Jareb tries to provoke Vireo into anger, hoping that he will become rash in his decision-making. But Vireo remains silent, his focus unwavering. And so, I continue to lie in wait, biding my time, and preparing for the moment when I can exact my revenge on the friend who has betrayed me.

My anticipation and anger swell within me as Vireo approaches the unconscious form of Laith, our fellow captive. I can feel my muscles tense, the desire for retribution surging like a raging storm. Each of Vireo's movements only serves to stoke the flames of my hatred, reminding me of Morgana's words and the pain I've suffered. My heart pounds in my chest, the drumbeat of war echoing in my ears. I clench my fists, knuckles white, barely restraining the urge to lash out. All the while, I wait, poised like a coiled serpent, ready to strike when the moment is right.

Vireo moves towards me, kneeling by my side. "Are you okay, my friend?" He places his hand on my shoulder in a feeble attempt to comfort me. Vireo looks me over, then back at Laith. Confusion crosses his face as he realises that, unlike Laith, I am not covered in blood or in poor shape.

Taking a deep breath, I come to life, surprising Vireo. "I am fine, brother, no thanks to you." I push him back forcefully before rising to my full height, the shackles around me now loose and unbinding.

"Lek?" Vireo lowers the fabric covering his face. "What is this?"

"For too long, we have lived in that blasted forest, living off stolen goods like common folk. You have brought shame to our houses, a shame that I cannot bear any longer."

Vireo looks truly shocked by my words, coming from his second in command and best friend. His face reveals the pain of this ultimate betrayal. "No, this can't be, Lek. Have you lost your mind?" He looks distraught at the scene unfolding.

"I can tell you my mind is clear," I respond, pressing my hands into the soft dirt in front of me to reveal my great axe hidden beneath.

With an almighty roar, I charge at Vireo, my anger towards him burning like a raging inferno. I never thought I would see the day when I'd turn against him but now all I have is a anger fuelled by hatred. Using my shoulder, I smash into Vireo, sending him barrel-rolling backward, a cloud of dirt forming around us. I grab him by the scruff of his cloak and hurl him even further back, more dirt spitting into the air and engulfing the surrounding area.

Through the cloud of dust, I can barely make out Vireo's form lying on the ground. The betrayal he must feel right now fills me with bitter satisfaction. "Brother, what are you doing? You need not do this?!" Vireo pleads, desperation tinging his voice.

"You are no longer my brother," I snarl back, raising my great axe above my head and bringing it crashing down towards Vireo with a furious roar. Vireo narrowly manages to roll out of the way.

"Brother, I do not wish to fight you!" Vireo stands with his hands up, a sign that he does not wish to engage with me, his newfound enemy.

"Do not call me that!" I cry out as I swing my axe wildly at Vireo once more. This time, Vireo ducks beneath the blow before rolling out of the way of the next swing I take. "Fight me!" I snarl, my anger towards my former friend matching my own ferocity.

"I will not fight you, brother," Vireo continues to protest, his hands open and outstretched, pleading for peace.

"I will." A second, slimmer figure emerges from the dust cloud, her slender frame clad in leather armour and a dark red cloak. Gillam's long, dark hair is tied back, and as she fixes her gaze upon me. She stares at me with a mixture of hurt and rage, I can feel the weight of her disappointment in my betrayal.

Her eyes, usually filled with a quiet strength, now burn with a fiery intensity that sends a shiver down my spine. I can see the pain etched on her face, her jaw clenched tightly as she struggles to comprehend the depth of my treachery. And yet, despite the anger and hurt that radiates from her, she stands tall and determined, ready to defend Vireo and confront the monster I have become.

As I grip the handle of my great axe, I can't help but feel a flicker of doubt, a pang of regret for the friend I've lost in Gillam. My hatred is towards Vireo not with her, yet she chooses to side with him without hesitation. My thoughts are quickly overtaken by the pulsing rage that fills my veins and the insidious whispers of Morgana's magic urging me to seek vengeance against Vireo and anyone who stands beside him.

ALSO BY A.P BESWICK

The Levanthria Series

A Forest Of Vanity And Valour

A Sea Of Sorrow And Scorn

A Kingdom Of Courage And Cruelty

A Stone Of Destiny And Despair

Tales Of Levanthria

A House Of Powder And Plot

A Frost Of Fear And Fortitude

A Frost Of Feathers And Deceit

Coming in 2024

The Ballad Of The Borag-I

A War Of Chaos And Fury - Part 1

A War Of Chaos And Fury - Part 2

You Can Check Out My Books at

MY STORE

AMAZON

Also by Cara Clare

The Phoenix Prophecy

Nova

Blaze

Ashes

Embers

Flames

Fire Bird

Blood

Ice

Coming Soon

Snow